MIDNIGHT INTRUDER

Longarm threw a hard left hook with his empty hand and sent the much smaller intruder across the bed and into a far corner to just sprawl there, limp as a rag doll.

He circled around the foot of the bed, revolver still in hand, to softly call out, "I'm coming, Short Stuff, and now we're going to have us some man-to-man talk." Then he saw who and what he'd just decked and said, "Oh . . . sorry, Ma'am."

The slim athletic-looking brunette in the mannish blue denim jeans and jacket sat up straight and said, "You cut my lip, you son of a bitch!"

- TABOR EVANS -

LONGARM

AND THE KILLER'S SHADOW

JOVE BOOKS, NEW YORK

LONGARM AND THE KILLER'S SHADOW

A Jove Book / published by arrangement with
the author

PRINTING HISTORY
Jove edition / January 1991

ISBN: 0-515-10494-9

10 9 8 7 6 5 4 3 2 1

LONGARM

AND THE
KILLER'S SHADOW

Chapter 1

Vernon Mankiller of the Cherokee Police was sort of killed by a prairie puff adder he encountered on the west bank of the Boxelder in Adams County, Colorado, during the April greenup when such critters tend to get more active amid the soapweed and buffalo grass of the High Plains.

Mankiller's untimely end was witnessed by his fellow peace officer, U.S. Deputy Marshal Custis Long of the Denver district court, who would later state in his written report that he doubted the snake had meant the fool Indian any harm to begin with and it couldn't have harmed anything bigger than, say, a sow bug if it had meant to. For a prairie puff adder sort of resembles a cross between a spitting cobra and an earthworm, with the ferocious looks and brag of the former and the size and venom of the latter.

Events leading up to the disastrous encounter in Colorado had commenced six hundred miles away in the Cherokee Strip of the Indian Nation, where Bart and Festus Larkin, along with the Wade brothers, had robbed the Sallisaw Agency, killing one white and two Indians in the process before compounding their felony by lighting out on U.S.

Cavalry mounts they'd stolen from Fort Smith.

An eight-man squad of uniformed Cherokee Police had trailed the not-too-bright quartet across the generally open range to just north-east of Denver without much trouble. But once the gang had gone to ground in an abandoned homesteader's soddy on the banks of the Boxelder, it had occurred to the somewhat brighter Indians that a shootout with whites this far from home could lead to all sorts of misunderstandings in a part of the West where memories of the last Cheyenne scare were still fresh. So their leader, Sergeant Ross Twopipes, had wired the Denver district court from the nearby trail town of Watkins, requesting federal backup before moving in, and U.S. Marshal William Vail had sent a five-man diamond of his own deputies under the command of his senior deputy, Custis Long, known to friend and foe alike as Longarm.

Longarm and his own boys hopped a freight train out of Denver to get off at Watkins and ride the last six or eight miles along the Boxelder aboard livery nags they hired right across from the cattle chutes. They found the Cherokee camped by the broad but shallow Boxelder in a clump of cottonwood and chokecherry about a mile from the abandoned homestead the gang was using as a hideout. They might have hidden better there had they not taken turns riding into Watkins to admire a soiled dove who figured the bounty on four federal wants had to be worth more than her own skinny ass would fetch on the open market these days.

Since the white lawmen met up with the Indian lawmen early of a bright and crispy Wednesday morn, Longarm suggested and Twopipes agreed they might as well just get it over with. So the thirteen of them rode north along the Boxelder, screened by the high banks and brush to their left, until they figured they'd pushed their luck and covered far enough on horseback. They dismounted to tether their ponies in some streamside brush a furlong south of the

2

hideout and ease in the rest of the way afoot with their saddle guns at port arms. Longarm and his boys packed mostly Winchester .44's, while the Indians still seemed to favor the older but lethal-as-ever Spencer .52. The Spencer carbine only packed seven rounds in its magazine, but when even one of those hit a man he sort of lost interest in anything else he'd been planning in the near future.

The Cherokee had already scouted the holed-up owlhoot riders before wiring for backup. So when Sergeant Twopipes announced they were about in position Longarm felt no call to doubt him. He turned to his own men and said, "Listen tight and let's get it right the first time. I want Smiley and Dutch down on the far left. Guilfoyle, you and Kelly move up to the right flank. That way, any curious cowhands who might ride on the sound of gunshots ought to see pale faces sporting badges before they notice these infernal redskins busting window glass. Otherwise, Sergeant Twopipes here gets to run the show as we move in. The rascals we'll be moving in on, Lord willing and the creeks don't rise, owe the Cherokee Nation a rope dance. So it's up to our guests here to call the tune, hear?"

Twopipes looked pleased but said, "Hear me, Longarm. You just said we were guests of your district court. You know this country better than we do too. You tell us what to do about those bad white boys and we will do it. I have spoken."

Longarm knew that meant the somewhat older Indian didn't want to argue about it and, meanwhile, the more time the law gave idle hands, the more mischief those hands could get into. So Longarm nodded, took off his tweed frock coat, and hung it on a chokecherry limb to head up the steep sandy bank in his shirtsleeves, Winchester loaded and locked across his broad chest, as he softly called, "Spread out and don't nobody raise his fool head too high whilst we study on this situation a mite."

A few seconds later he had his elbows hooked over the edge with the Winchester cradled in his arms and some

3

soapweed screening his head from the ominously silent soddy an easy rifle shot to the west. Wanting to see more, Longarm removed his dark pancaked Stetson and lay it to one side in the grass before craning his bare head a bit higher. Sergeant Twopipes, reclining just to Longarm's left, stayed put as he remarked, "Those four ponies in the corral just south of the soddy are it. You can see they have a fifty-foot dash from the nearest door to the corral. Even if they made it, they would have to ride out bareback across a flat field of fire for, what, half a mile?"

Longarm pursed his lips thoughtfully and decided, "I doubt I'd do her that way if I was in their fix. No offense, but men have been known to miss a moving target at that range and, once I had me a pony betwixt my legs, I reckon I'd streak north-northeast at a sharp angle and get my own fool head down off the skyline. They might even hit the creek bed both ways, forcing us to split up too. Have you any notion at all about the final destination those four scamps could have in mind?"

The Indian lawman shook his head morosely and replied, "I don't think their leader, Bart Larkin, plans more than a day ahead. Hear me, they have been riding north by northwest ever since we have been trailing them from Sallisaw. I don't think they know why either."

Longarm reached absently for a cheroot, decided this would be a stupid time to smoke, and mused aloud, "I dunno. Not even a bee is inclined to beeline like that unless it has some destination in mind, Sarge. But why are we just guessing when all we have to do is *ask* the sons of bitches, providing we can take 'em alive?"

Suiting actions to his words, Longarm braced the butt plate of his Winchester against his right shoulder and sighted on one of the army mounts in the corral as he flicked off the safety lock. Ross Twopipes had tracked down mounted outlaws in his time as well. So he didn't ask why but cocked his Spencer, muttering, "Hear me, I wish there was another way."

It was just about then that the aforementioned and unfortunate Vernon Mankiller, to Longarm's right, decided to get killed by that prairie puff adder. The bitty snake had only decided to bluff the big brown face looming over it by puffing and hissing as puff adders are inclined to when anything bigger than a horsefly scares them shitless. The results scared Vernon Mankiller way more than it should have scared any full-grown man of any race. For poor Mankiller was one of those natural snake-shunners who tends to leap before he looks. He sprang to his feet, screaming, "Snake! Snake! Snake!" until a rifle squibbed in the distance and the unfortunate Mankiller flew backward with a big red rose of blood and lung tissue pinned to the front of his dark blue shirt.

That inspired all the other lawmen up and down the bank to pepper the soddy with return fire. Longarm dropped the four ponies in the nearby pole corral before he ordered a cease-fire with a loud string of curses that finally got through to the last of the lawmen as he was reloading. When they heard another shot ring out inside the shot-up soddy, Longarm called, warningly, "Hold your fire, boys. There's nobody worth shooting at near window one."

As if to prove him right a mournful voice from the soddy called out to them through the slowly settling dust. "That was surely a shitty way to treat our ponies, Longarm! What makes you so mean, anyways?"

Longarm called back, "Pissants like you, for openers. You know why we had to make sure you couldn't ride out. To whom might I have the honor and who told you who I was, Pissant?"

The trapped outlaw called back, "I'd be Bart Larkin. My baby brother, Festus, caught a round in his poor skinny arm just now, and you'll no doubt be pleased to hear neither Rafe nor Lem are with us no more. It was Lem Wade as gunned that Indian agent down in the Cherokee Strip last April, and his brother, Rafe, was the one as got that Indian boy just now. Is the fool Cherokee entirely dead?"

Longarm shot a morose glance over to his right and called back, "Yep. Unless you're hoping to make it a score of four to one, you'd best toss your guns ahead and come on out with your hands up, now."

Bart Larkin chuckled indulgently and replied, "Yep, you're the one called Longarm. They told us we could expect to meet up with you in these parts, and they say you're a man of your words as well as mean enough to shoot a poor boy's pony!"

Longarm called back, "Flattery won't get you half as much as coming out of there before we come in with a fusillade of covering fire. So what's your pleasure, Larkin?"

The trapped outlaw called back, "A deal. Your word neither me nor my baby brother, Festus, will have to hang for any past misunderstandings."

Longarm could only laugh and confided to the Indian beside him, "*Loco en la cabeza,* or drunk." Then he called out, louder, "We're neither your judge nor jury out here, Bart. You know we ain't about to let you go, and it ain't for us to say what they decide at your trial, if you'd like to have one. To tell the truth, we don't give a shit whether we take you back to town dead or alive."

The boxed-in outlaw replied, "Me and Festus would rather go on living if it's all the same with you. What if we was to turn state's evidence?"

Longarm asked, sincerely, "Against who, about what? I can't see your dead confederates standing trial for shit, and whether it was you or them as gunned four federal employees within recent memory, they hang you just as high as an accessory to Murder in the First."

The two brothers trapped in the soddy hadn't enjoyed those words of cheer, judging from the long silence that followed. Longarm got that cheroot out, now, and lit it, head still low, before he called out, not unkindly, "Figuring all the paperwork and appeals, even after they find you guilty, you boys figure to last until at least Halloween, if you'd like to come on out now. Make us come in after you and I can

6

promise you'll never see the sun go down this evening."

"I needs a doc for this awesome wound!" another voice called back, higher-pitched and far less defiant.

So Longarm said, "Come on out then, and let your big brother be the hero of the family, Festus."

But it was Bart who answered, defiantly. "You ain't heard my proposition yet, Longarm. What if I was to tell you why we helt up that allotment office down to the Cherokee Strip, for openers?"

Longarm snorted in disgust and shot back, "That won't buy you a match stem in this game, let alone a chip. You robbed the Cherokee for the simple reason they had money in that safe at Sallisaw. What in thunder's so mysterious about that?"

"Don't you want to know why we wanted that money?" Larkin answered in a foxy-grandpa tone.

To which Longarm could only reply, in a tone of sheer disgust, "We know how you spent some of the money, you poor simp. The whore in town you were beating down for group rates was the one as told us where you were holed up when you weren't in her cut-rate hole." He added, not unkindly, "Let that be a lesson to you boys about gals. Many an owlhoot rider's been turned in by a woman he's been treating generous. Treat one cheap and she'll turn on you every time."

Bart called back, impatiently, "We figured somebody in Watkins must have told you boys where we was. Getting back to our reasons for robbing them redskins, what if I was to tell you it was for our college tuition?"

That sounded so dumb that Longarm simply laughed. Down the firing line to his left the deputy called Dutch, known for his sardonic sense of humor as well as his nasty temper, called out, "What were you boys figuring to study on in college, advanced ass-wipin' or how to make change for a nickel without moving your lips?"

Bart Larkin replied, defensively, "Advanced crimination or the committing of crimes without getting caught."

7

Longarm yelled at Dutch to stay out of it and remarked to Larkin that he made a certain amount of sense, adding, "Lord knows you boys sure must have started out self-taught. Are you saying you know of some sort of school as gives degrees in, let's say, highway robbery?"

Larkin sounded sincere as he shot back, "Train robbery was what we had in mind. That's where the real money is. I hope you've heard of Jethro Markham, the unreconstructed Rebel raider as taught the Reno brothers the art of stopping trains, just after the war betwixt the states?"

Longarm grimaced, blew smoke out both nostrils, and yelled, "Now I know you're only playing for time, pissant. The Reno gang was before my time with the Justice Department. But I have come across some of their past associates from time to time, and the last I heard of old Professor Markham, he could have used more train-robbing lessons his own self. He was nailed by the Pinkertons back in the early seventies, and they not only locked him up but threw away the key. He bought Life at Hard, speaking of turning state's evidence and . . . Come to study on it, I do believe he died in his dreary prison cell a year or more ago. Any of you other boys recall that update we got on the poor old cuss?"

Deputy Smiley, who never smiled, called up the line as morosely as ever. "Iowa State Prison, last November. I remember the flyer on the bulletin board because I shacked up with a part-Crow waitress in Sioux City one time. Don't never do that if your own Indian blood happens to be Pawnee."

Longarm smiled softly at the picture and never asked why. Smiley was a good old boy, but there did seem to be something about Pawnee that irritated just about everyone else, red and white alike.

The shady past of his fellow deputy wasn't at all important to anyone else around there. So Longarm called back, "You'll have to do better than old train robbers who've already paid their just debts to society, Bart. I don't suppose

8

you'd know where Frank and Jesse might be hiding out this season, eh?"

"Jethro Markham's still alive and he's out," the killer in the soddy insisted, adding, "He'd be the first who'd agree with you about them few mistakes as got him caught that time. He's had many a moon to study on the way he should have done it and could have done it, had he knowed then what he knows now."

Longarm didn't answer. As he'd hoped, the cornered rat on the far side of the shot-up sod wall insisted, pleadingly, "Me and my baby brother are bitty fish next to the big one I'm offering to fry for you, Longarm. I know we done wrong and we're willing to do some time for it, as long as we can save our necks."

Longarm just blew a thoughtful smoke ring.

Bart Larkin yelled, "Damn it, Longarm, the professor's fixing to set up classes, like I already told you, and then, once he gets a whole passel of younger riders educated better than the Reno and James boys put together, he aims to show you and your'n a crime spree as will have you convinced that deal Grant made with Lee at Appomattox never happened!"

Sergeant Twopipes grumbled, "Hear me, they are stalling, stalling. What are we waiting for? I am not afraid to die, and even if I was, they just killed one of my men!"

Longarm nodded amiably but said, "It ain't halfways to noon yet. They're likely out to buy time, like you say. Meanwhile neither of 'em can get away and at least one of 'em needs a doctor more than you, me, or even Mankiller. I'd like to see what else we can get out of 'em."

Suiting action to words he called out, "All right. I'll bite. Tell us where this institute of low-down education might be and I'll see what I can do for you."

It didn't work. Bart Larkin called back, "I want your word neither me nor Festus here will hang."

Longarm swore softly and said, "You know I only work here, damn it. I can tell Judge Dickerson of the Denver

9

district court I owe you boys a favor. It's up to him whether he thinks he owes me any."

Bart called back, "What if you was to tell the judge you'd hand in your badge and leave him and Colorado at the mercy of all the other boys like us on the day he made either one of us do the rope dance?"

Longarm took a thoughtful drag on his cheroot, then called their bluff with, "I could promise you that much. That's not saying anyone else will give a damn if I go or stay."

There was a long interval of muffled conversation inside the soddy as, closer to Longarm by far, Twopipes grumbled, "Hear me, I don't like the way this deal seems to be going. How do we know it was one of the others, and not the one you're dealing with, who shot Mankiller just a few minutes ago?"

Longarm replied, "We don't. Meanwhile, on the outside chance the little shit may really put us on to someone bigger, I mean to promise him as much and no more than I have to."

Before Twopipes could answer Longarm called out, gruffly, "I got me some impatient sidekicks out here and the sun's getting hotter as it rises, boy. If you want to ride back to town with us alive you'd best get cracking!"

Bart called back, "Hold your damned fire. I got me a scared baby brother here. We have your word you'll turn in your badge and gun if that infernal judge of your'n won't go along with, say, Twenty with Time?"

Longarm said a dreadful thing about outlaws in general and their mothers in particular before he replied, "I keep my gun, it's personal property, and you'll be lucky to get off with Life at Hard no matter what I threaten Judge Dickerson with. That's my final offer. Come out friendly or we're coming in mean!"

So a few moments later four carbines and six pistols sailed out the shot-up soddy door, followed by the two shabby and sheepish survivors. Bart Larkin had both hands up. Festus was hugging his bloody right sleeve to his chest as if it were a dying infant. Longarm called out to let the little pissant live.

As he and Twopipes rose from their prone positions in the weeds the Indian lawman grumbled, "Hear me, this is wrong and you know it, Longarm. They have killed one of your people and three of mine. If your Denver judge lets them off with anything less than the rope, I am going to be very cross with him too!"

Longarm muttered, "Keep it down to a roar and let's eat this apple a bite at a time. I want to get as much as I can out of the horse's ass older brother before he wises up."

The Cherokee shot Longarm a thoughtful frown and demanded, "Are you saying you don't mean to put in a good word for them with that judge you know?"

Longarm shook his head and replied, "I never break my word, unless I have to, and in this case, praise the Lord, I don't have to. I'll be proud to ask Judge Dickerson not to hang those boys, once we get 'em back to Denver."

The Indian growled, "I must have my fingers in my ears. Your words don't make any sense. First you seem to agree they deserve to hang, and then you say you are going to ask the judge not to hang them?"

Longarm nodded and murmured, "I have to. You heard me promise. But I fail to see how Judge Dickerson on the Denver district court could hang either of 'em if he wanted to."

As the Indian stared thunderstruck Longarm added, "Correct me if I'm wrong, but you surely never lit out after four white men without proper arrest warrants, right?"

Twopipes snorted in disgust and replied, "You know we're not allowed to arrest white men off Indian land without a federal warrant signed by a white magistrate and . . . Oh, I see what you mean."

Longarm grinned back at the grinning Indian and softly whispered, "Hold the thought and let's hope *they* don't. What kind of papers do you pack on 'em, Murder in the

First signed by old Isaac Parker down in Fort Smith?"

Twopipes chuckled and replied, " They're right about you being a man of your word. But hear me, they are right about how mean you can be to outlaws too!"

Chapter 2

It was well after sundown by the time they had the Larkin boys back in Denver, with some unpleasant surprises still in store for them, come Thursday morn before Judge Dickerson. Meanwhile Longarm had been taking notes all the way back from that soddy, and being that a certain young matron at the Arvada Orphan Asylum was still sore at him about that redheaded barmaid at the Parthenon, while the redhead was still in love with that worthless gambling man, and a certain young widow woman up on Capitol Hill was entertaining kin from back East, Longarm made the best of a bad situation by letting himself into the office in the federal building after hours and typing up a terser and more readable report from his penciled notes.

He left what Bart Larkin had had to say about Professor Jethro Markham and his college for crime on the already cluttered desk of his boss, Marshal Billy Vail, before letting himself out and locking up again. As he strode for the stairwell along the dark and gloomy marble corridor, reflecting that the night was still young and he was a mite old for masturbation, a door popped open ahead of him to spill lamplight and Miss Bubbles, from the stenographers' pool, in his path.

The perky plump blonde had a more sensible name than Bubbles, of course, if any man who grinned at her could ever remember it. But even she seemed to approve of the nickname that fit her so well. She likely looked in the mirror every time she powdered her little button nose or brushed more stove-blacking on her fluttersome eyelashes. She was fluttering them ferociously as she confided, "Ooh, you startled me, Custis. What are you doing up here so late, you mean thing?"

He said, "Catching up on some paperwork. Have I done something mean to you, Miss Bubbles?"

She pouted. "No, and I'm mighty vexed at you about that. I understand it's not discreet for two folk who work in the same building to get, ah, indiscreet with one another. But honestly, what harm can just another teeny-weeny slice do once the loaf's been cut so grand on that chesterfield sofa down the hall, Lover Lamb?"

Longarm sighed and confided, "There's no such thing as just another slice when it comes to your sweet loaf and you know it. Being indiscreet with you is sort of like eating peanuts. There's just no way a man's going to be satisfied with one and, damn it, Miss Bubbles, you know we'd have wound up getting caught if we hadn't agreed to quit whilst we was ahead."

She giggled and said, "I know. I like to wet myself the time that night watchman rattled the door latch just as we was coming on the far side. Hold the thought. I got to use the crapper down the hall and as soon as I get back . . . "

He started to protest her indelicate suggestion. Then he had a better idea and asked, "Do you still type and file for the B.L.M., you pretty little thing?"

She said, "I type and file for damn near every federal office in this damned federal building, save for you stuffy lawmen and . . . can't it wait, Custis? If I don't tinkle yonder, I figure to tinkle all over your boots and mine!"

He laughed and let her go. As soon as she was out of sight he told himself, sternly, "If you had a lick of sense you'd haul ass afore she gets back, you horny rascal!"

He reached for a smoke instead. For he knew she was really going to be sore if he lit out on her even as she was no doubt preparing for safe passion in the crapper down the hall. And while he knew it was wrong to mess with stuff where he worked, he did have a valid reason for, well, putting his head together with a fellow federal employee who could get him into the land-office files if he asked real nice.

He'd only enjoyed a few drags on his cheroot before Miss Bubbles returned, her hair unpinned and a wicked gleam in her big blue eyes. She said, "There's a really plush sofa in the inner office, dear."

But he shook his head and said, "There's a swell tufted leather job in the land office too. If we're going to be indiscreet some more, Miss Bubbles, I'll thank you to let me combine some business with pleasure."

She sighed and said, "Oh, pooh, I might have known you weren't just after my body. Let me trim the lamps in this office then. What are you so hot for in the land office, present company excluded?"

He stood in the doorway as she put out the oil lamps in the office she'd wanted to drag him into. He told her, "This time I promise I'll only be a minute in the file room. This morning we picked up some young owlhoot riders who'd ridden far and straight as honeybees for an abandoned homestead no more than twenty miles from here. I naturally asked how in thunder they'd known about the place. They told me a recent pal, Rafe Wade, had led them there from the Indian Nation. I couldn't ask Rafe. He caught a bullet with his head shortly after a Cherokee on our side caught one with his chest."

Miss Bubbles, having plunged the office behind her into total darkness, herded him out into the almost-as-gloomy corridor, coyly confiding, "Let's hurry. I'm just gushing

15

for you-know-what and to tell the truth, I don't care why you want to get into the homestead files, as long as you want to get in me!"

So he followed her on down to the land office and did. She was so hot by this time that she'd shucked her summer-weight dress and was writhing in anticipation on the tufted leather chesterfield by the time he'd made sure the office door was securely latched on the inside. She cursed at him as if he were an army mule as he took the time to take off all his own duds, save for the socks. But once they were at it, jay-naked on the waiting-room furniture, she allowed as all was forgiven as she locked her striped cotton stockings and high-button shoes around the nape of his neck. Miss Bubbles was sort of limber as well as passionate. Longarm knew he'd be ashamed of himself in the morning for ignoring his own policy against messing with the gals at work, but meanwhile he'd been right about her being sort of like peanuts. He had to come in her three times, the last time dog-style across the reception desk, before she allowed she could use a breather or at least a smoke.

He found his rumpled vest in a far corner, got out a cheroot and some waterproof matches, and got it going for the both of them as they cooled off a bit sitting side by side, bare-ass, on the sofa. Then, leaving her the cheroot in the romantic light of an office illuminated only by the street lamp just outside one window, Longarm rose with the matches to amble into the smaller room they kept the files in. As he recalled from before, there was a wall fixture. He struck a match and lit it. Then, taking his time as he scanned the mental map he'd drawn in his own head that afternoon, he decided he needed something better than that and hauled out one of the big flat shallow drawers they kept the county plats in. After that it was a simple matter to locate the plat number that fit that lonesome as well as abandoned soddy just north of Watkins on the Boxelder.

Longarm hated paper-trailing. That was one of the reasons he was good at it. It only took him a few more minutes to find the original homestead claim in the fortunately cross-indexed files, and once he had, he laughed so loud Miss Bubbles ran in, naked above the garters with the cheroot gripped in her teeth, to warn him, "Not so loud. And what's so funny, you maniac?"

He shoved the file drawer neatly shut, having no need to save or copy anything, this time, and confided, "I have just proven an outlaw I had down as a liar could have been telling me the truth. My fool notes are out yonder with my duds, wherever my fool duds may be, but the abandoned homestead I was interested in reverted to public land a few years back when a nester called Paget, Hiram Paget, wound up in the Iowa State Prison afore he could prove his homestead claim in Colorado."

Miss Bubbles repressed a yawn and said, "That sure sounds interesting, and speaking of interesting, there's a notion that's popped into my head more than once as I was filing otherwise tedious papers in bottom drawers."

He could only reply with a puzzled smile. Miss Bubbles handed him the cheroot, turned her back to him, and bent over, way over, to pull out a file drawer and brace her upper body's weight on it, stiff-elbowed. The admirable view of her bubbly derriere inspired a certain stiffness on Longarm's part, even before she shot him an arch look over one bare rounded shoulder and roguishly inquired, "Would you like to stake a claim anywhere around here?"

He chuckled fondly down at her delightful invitation, allowed he knew exactly where he wanted his old stake, placed a palm on each firmly fleshed round hip, and stepped up to take his proper place at bat. As he hauled her on like a throbbing wet glove she bit her lower lip and hissed, "Ooh, that feels so wild and wicked! I'm so glad you wanted to come in here!"

He said, "Me too. Hiram Paget was Jethro Markham's cell mate in the Iowa State Prison. So that answers how some would-be pupils of the good Professor Markham might have known an unproven homestead was standing empty

17

but still roofed on the high plains of Colorado. Their tale of Markham's escape from said prison is commencing to make a mite more sense, albeit I can't get it down without more than one good pinch of salt."

She protested, wigwagging her rounded rump for emphasis, "Never mind anyone else's tail, dammit! My tail feels wild indeed and I wish you'd do it faster so's I could finish this way before I faint. All the blood seems to be rushing to my head and if you don't want me passing out on you . . ."

He shushed her with a thrust that made her gasp with delight as he assured her the blood was rushing to his head too, and suggested they finish with her bare elbows braced on top of the filing cabinet instead. She protested that he wouldn't be able to get it in as far that way. But once he had her bare back up against his heaving chest she allowed, with her own chest heaving, it was in her far enough.

The next morning, after the hearty breakfast it took to get his legs working right again, Longarm stopped at the downtown office of the *Rocky Mountain News* on his way to his own. The *Rocky Mountain News* was a bit smaller but much older than its rival, the *Denver Post*. So whenever Longarm wanted to dig really stale stuff out of a newspaper morgue, he naturally thought first of an outfit without a Denver to its masthead. The *Rocky Mountain News* had been in business when Denver was still the mining camp of Cherry Creek.

The old geezer you had to ask had doubtless been of voting age when Francis Parkman had first noted that otherwise uninteresting creek lined with chokecherries back in '46. It wouldn't have been polite to ask. To hear him brag, he'd panned the second if not the first gold nugget over in Cherry Creek before the first frame shithouse was erected in these parts, circa 1857.

They called the geezer Pop. Longarm offered the old-timer a cheroot, even though they both knew he preferred to chew in his world of oily printer's ink thinned with naphtha. Pop put the cheroot away for after work, and warned Longarm not to strike a match in there either. So Longarm decided he'd have his own smoke later, with coffee and apple pie, and got down to brass tacks.

As he'd hoped, Pop recalled the sad story of Hiram Paget, a good old Colorado boy gone wrong, in Pop's opinion. As he led the way back to the morgue Pop said, "I recall the story well because of all the mail we got on Paget and the wages of being soft on Southern sons of bitches. Colorado was ferociously Union during the war and Paget was at best a Galvanized Yankee. You heard about them, of course?"

Longarm nodded and replied, "Read about 'em. We're talking about them Confederate prisoners of war the Union Army got to ride against Little Crow that time, ain't we?"

Pop said, "Yep, the pesky Sioux knew Johnny Reb had the Union Army too busy to chase fool redskins. What they never figured on was Johnny Rebs locked up in the Sandusky stockade feeling just as awful about white women and children getting scalpt."

By now they'd entered the musty morgue lined with stacks of dusty filing cabinets. Pop slid one open, saying, "It's all in here. All we got on Hiram Paget at any rate. After fighting the Sioux for the Union and getting a Yankee discharge at the end of the war, he never did return to his native land of Alabam'. Lincoln had signed the Homestead Act about the same time he was setting free the slaves. But Paget never filed on that quarter section up near Watkins until the stock market crash of '73 cost him his job with the railroad."

Pop hauled out a manila folder, placed it atop the cabinet between them, and added, "Read it and weep. Poor bastard had managed to hang on for almost the full five years when he heard of another railroading opportunity over near Sioux City and got caught."

Longarm thanked the old-timer with a nod and opened the dusty dossier. Pop said he had to get back to the salt mines and warned Longarm what he'd do to any fresh young

19

whippersnapper who failed to put things back alphabetical when he was dammit done with 'em.

In point of fact, Longarm only jotted down a dozen lines or less before he decided the *Rocky Mountain News* neither made a total liar out of Bart Larkin nor confirmed his story about Professor Jethro Markham in detail.

Homesteading Hiram Paget had in fact taken part in a half-ass attempt at stopping the Chicago & North Western Express between the Little Sioux and Big Sioux rivers. Nobody had been hurt, and it appeared Hiram's only part in the dumb stunt had involved holding the horses for his fellow assholes in a nearby cornfield. That explained how the gang had known nobody else would have claimed the poor simp's soddy. Despite some letters to the editor, the State of Iowa had let Hiram Paget off with Two at Hard in exchange for his guilty plea and doubtless-sincere apology. There was nothing on file about Paget getting out. But Longarm knew that barring bad behavior, they'd have cut him loose with the usual two dollars and cheap suit by now, had he lived.

Longarm put all they had on Paget back in the drawer and then, just in case, he tried for anything they had on Jethro Markham. They didn't have anything. That was no mystery. Markham had ridden for the South, Larkin had said, as a guerrilla who specialized in Union payrolls traveling by rail. Whether he'd later taught the skills involved to a Union deserter called Frank Reno or not, that first rash of postwar train robberies had commenced around Seymour, Indiana, and neither Markham nor the Reno boys nor, come to think about it, the James and Younger boys had ever robbed a train this far west. Bart Larkin had said Markham, serving Life at Hard, had simply changed places with Hiram Paget a few short hours before Paget was due to walk out the front gate like a big-ass bird. That the two train robbers had met up in the same prison, one serving short and the other long, went down easy enough, even without proof. It was when Paget died natural of a heart-stroke just before they were fixing to turn him loose that the story got to sounding so unbelievable.

Thanking Pop on his way out, Longarm ambled on to the federal building and up to Marshal Vail's office. By now it was just a bit late in the workday, even for Longarm, so young Henry, the prissy-looking dude who played the typewriter out front, shot Longarm one of those "You're wanted in the principal's office!" looks and told him the boss wanted to see him when and if he ever showed up around there again.

Longarm sighed and said, "You don't have to look as if you're coming in your pants, Henry," and paused to light a fresh cheroot before he went on back to face the music. He knew that every time he lit up in front of Billy Vail the old fart tended to tell him he smoked too much.

This was likely true but hardly just, coming from a man who smoked what Longarm suspected of being lengths of greasewood root cured in sheep-dip. As he entered Vail's oak-paneled inner sanctum, as if to prove him right, the much older, much shorter, and much heftier Billy Vail blew a thunderhead of pungent cigar smoke at him and announced from somewhere in its swirling depths, "I figured you might show up in time for lunch. You missed all the swell things Bart Larkin had to say about you and your mother as we were seeing him off to Fort Smith with those Cherokee Police. His brother, Festus, is still over to County General. The sawbones says it would likely kill him if we sent him that far to hang in his condition. A soft-nosed .52 sure smarts when it flattens out against bone. By the way, was anyone on our side packing a .36?"

Longarm sat uninvited in the one decent chair on his side of the marshal's cluttered desk and answered, "Nope. Me and the other white boys all load both our saddle guns and side arms .44−40 like you tell everyone who rides for you. The Indians packed mostly .52 Spencers and .45 Army Schofields. Is there any point to this, Billy?"

Vail said, "Nope. Bart Larkin must have been the one who gunned both Lem and Rafe Wade with his .36 Patterson Conversion. Got the coroner's report on that just after we saw the murderous cuss off at the depot. So much for his plaintive tale about it being the older and meaner Wade boys who led him and his baby brother astray."

Longarm leaned back more comfortably as he said, "Judge Parker over in Fort Smith is going to throw the book at 'em no matter who shot whom with what, or why. Did you get the chance to read the report I typed up about the conversation I had with old Bart, before he decided I was a mother-fucker?"

Vail said, "I did. Have you ever heard the one about the Three Little Pigs and the Big Bad Wolf? Jethro Markham died of natural causes in the Iowa State Prison, along about the middle of winter last year. They buried him more recently, on the prison grounds, on account of you just can't dig too deep in Iowa before the spring thaw."

Longarm blew some thinner and much sweeter-smelling tobacco smoke back at Vail in self-defense and said, "According to Bart Larkin, it was old Hiram Paget who died last winter, in an underheated cell block where everyone had to bundle up pretty good. I just came from the morgue of the *Rocky Mountain News*. There really was a Hiram Paget doing time with Markham. He was due to get out around election time this fall. Say he was a model prisoner and they were about to let him out after he'd served a little more than two thirds of his sentence. Then say he died, or somebody helped him die without leaving too many marks on the body, and then say—"

"There was this pretty little thing called Snow White," Vail cut in with a wave of his magic cigar. "She managed to stay pure even though she was shacked up with seven dirty old men, and then a wicked witch poisoned her, only that didn't matter on account of this here prince came along to make love to a corpse and . . . Jesus H. Christ, old son, there simply ain't no way a man serving Life at Hard is going to get a handshake and a two-dollar bill off a sober warden and walk out the front gate as another prisoner entirely!"

Longarm studied the ash on the tip of his cheroot, flicked some on the rug to discourage carpet mites and convince Vail he really ought to have some damned ashtrays on this side of the deak, and protested, "I read this book by Charlie Dickens one time, and who's to say they didn't have a copy in the prison library? It was this tale about two cities, and anyway, there's this one jasper in this French jailhouse, fixing to have his head lopped off any minute, only an otherwise useless drunk who admires the condemned man's wife and kids comes in as a visitor and swaps places with him. The guards didn't care, as long as they still had one gent in his cell and the one walking out had the proper papers on him, see?"

Vail grimaced and replied, "Hell, you can't expect infernal Frenchmen to guard as good as anyone in Iowa. I read that tale about the two cities, one time. Weren't those two pals exact doubles, like identical twins, and have you ever seen anyone in real life who comes that close to anyone he wasn't even related to?"

Longarm shook his head and said, "The two pals in that book didn't look like one another, albeit they might have been described much the same as to age, weight, and so forth on that prison pass. Don't forget that the guards in Iowa were called about a man dropping dead in the cell block in the wee small hours, long before anyone was supposed to get out on good behavior. A dead man's a dead man in poor light to anyone who only knew him casually and might feel uncomfortable in the close company of Mister Death. Say the guards on duty were told poor old Professor Jethro Markham had served his life sentence in full and at last. Then say the guards detailed some prisoners to tote the damned stiff to the infirmary, where, say, a trusty detailed as a corpse-washer was the only one who really needed a good look at a middle-aged cadaver of average appearance."

23

Vail wrinkled his nose and insisted, "No trusty escorts anyone to the front gate. If it's not the warden, it's usually the deputy warden who hands the released prisoner his papers, two dollars, and a few firm words on the perils of demon rum and dishonesty in general. Are you saying even a master crook who calls himself a professor could get by with anything as raw as that?"

Longarm shrugged and said, "It was Bart Larkin who said it. You just now said Markham had a rep for being a master crook, and if that won't work, let us not forget that many a lawman has been tempted to look the other way when the price was right."

Vail gasped and protested, "Longarm! That's a hell of a thing to say about the boys who run the Iowa State Prison!"

Longarm enjoyed another pull on his smoke and replied, "Wouldn't take all of 'em or even half of 'em, and I'm not suggesting anything as raw as Sheriff Henry Plummer and his deputies guarding stage lines by day and robbing 'em by night. Just give me one or two underpaid state employees bought off, or, hell, incompetent, and a heap of things fall smack in place, Boss."

Vail shook his bullet head and said, "Not hardly. Bart Larkin swears he had nothing to do with the death of one white and three Indian federal employees too. Even if he could be telling the truth, how in thunder would you go about proving one damned point?"

Longarm gripped the cheroot in his teeth to count on his fingers as he answered, "*Número uno,* neither the Larkin nor Wade brothers were Colorado riders. Yet they knew where Paget's abandoned homestead was. *Número dos,* they knew it would still be abandoned once they got there. How come, if Hiram Paget was released from prison last winter? According to the *Rocky Mountain News,* he'd about proven his homestead claim when he was arrested and sent to prison in Iowa. Without asking the legal department down the hall, I'd say nobody with a lick of sense would want to file on

24

a claim with a clouded title, and Paget could likely work something out with the land office, once he returned alive, to, say, fix the windows and drill in some barley."

Vail nodded soberly and said, "I'll concede you that chip. It does seem odd, now that you mention it, but what if Paget was just ashamed to come back to these parts as a convicted train robber? How much credit could he hope for on that window glass and seed you mentioned? It ain't as if a quarter section of marginal range on the High Plains was the alpha and omega of starting almost from scratch, you know."

Longarm nodded but said, "*Número tres,* the would-be pupils of the one and original Professor Jethro Markham would have no call to look up a loser such as Hiram Paget. Even assholes who'd steal army mounts and ride 'em cross-country in broad daylight ought to be able to see you don't take train-robbing lessons from a man who got caught the very first time he tried. So where were the four of 'em headed if it wasn't to enroll in Professor Markham's college of crime?"

"In a tumbledown soddy, just a hop, skip, and a jump from town?" Billy Vail demanded with a derisive eyebrow raised.

Longarm replied, "I naturally asked about that on the way back to Denver. Both brothers said they'd been told they'd be picked up by other associates of the professor, once it seemed clear they'd made it that far with their tuition fees, with nobody like you, me, or them pretty good Cherokee Police on their trail."

Vail grimaced and snubbed out his evil but, thankfully, almost-gone cigar as he growled, "In sum, dead end, whether they were shitting you or telling it to you true blue. What do you expect me to do about it, now that the whole world knows about the shootout and resultant capture out at that soddy—order you to stake that soddy out?"

Longarm nodded and replied, "That might not be as dumb a move as it sounds. I stake out mighty sneaky, and you

25

know what they say about crooks returning curious as cats."

Billy Vail demanded, "To what end, even if you drew the wages of a senior deputy to haunt abandoned homesteads? I sent you and the boys out there at the request of other federal lawmen in hot pursuit of outlaws wanted in another federal district. Said outlaws have all been killed or captured. What else do you want, egg in your beer?"

Longarm firmly replied, "I'd settle for a neater wrap-up. If there's anything at all to Bart Larkin's story about old Jethro Markham, we could be talking about a case of major malfeasance, gross incompetence, or both, on the part of other lawmen!"

Vail shook his bullet head and replied, "*Iowa State* lawmen, you mean. We're not even supposed to help Colorado keep its own state convicts under lock and key unless they ask us. I got a lot of shit atop this desk here, but I'll be fried once-over-lightly if I recall anything about anyone escaping from Iowa State Prison."

Longarm said, "Maybe they don't know they have the late Hiram Paget buried out back as Professor Jethro Markham. The body ain't been in the ground all that long, and if someone was to wire someone a tad higher on the totem pole . . . "

"Don't you dare!" roared Billy Vail, leaping to his feet behind his desk to do a little war dance around his swivel chair as he thundered, "To begin with, whatever they got buried out back has been down there long enough, now that the ground's been thawed a good six weeks, and if they was able to mix one middle-aged convict with another when both were still fresh—"

"Let's eat the apple a bite at a time," Longarm cut in with a thin smile. "No matter who they buried as Professor Jethro Markham, the one they turned loose as Hiram Paget is still above ground in a less disgusting condition. Once he's been picked up—"

"On what charge, county, state, or federal?" snapped Vail.

To which Longarm as insistently replied, "Suspicion. Any peace officer can run in anybody on suspicion, and unless he's got a damn good lawyer, hold him for seventy-two on the same. No matter who in blue blazes is running around right now with a prison release made out to Hiram Paget, both of 'em must have been photographed when they were arrested to begin with, right?"

Vail started to object. Then he brightened and replied, "By jimmies, if either half-ass train robber was tintyped by the Pinkerton railroad dicks, it won't matter whether anyone's fiddled with their prison files. You go ahead and wire 'em to send us some sepia-tones of both those rascals, if you've a mind to. But mind you, do it on your own time, during your lunch hour. I'll be damned if I'll have any of my help indulging in such long shots at the taxpayers' expense!"

Chapter 3

The Western Union office nearest the federal building was on the far side of the Parthenon Saloon, where the quality of the free lunch made up for the scandalous ten cents they charged for a schooner of needled beer. So once he'd gotten his wires off to the Des Moines branch of the Pinks, Longarm entered the Parthenon via a side door usually reserved for the more delicate comings and goings of the female clientele.

The Parthenon was too fancy-pants to serve anyone wearing skirts at the bar, with the possible exception of visiting Scotchmen, but lest any thirsty lady feel affronted or, God forbid, take her thirst to some rival establishment, the management provided comfortable and cozy private rooms to either side of the corridor that let a male or female customer enter around the corner from the main entrance.

Another nice thing about coming in that way was the walk it saved to the free-lunch counter, which was naturally set up a good hike from the swinging front doors any hungry pest might reel through. As Longarm noted he'd arrived a bit late for the deviled eggs he liked, but not too late for the pickled pigs' feet some held to be an acquired taste, or perversion, he saw a familiar figure in a checked suit. Crawford of the *Denver Post* spotted Longarm about the same time, blinked in surprise, and called out, "Howdy, Judge Dickerson. You might be able to help us out here, seeing you work over at the federal building."

Now, since Crawford was hardly fat enough, yet, to qualify as an "us," Longarm figured it was safe to assume the much leaner and hungrier-looking individual at the lunch counter with him had to be part of the mystery. The stranger was dressed in faded denim with a tan canvas duster over his gun arm. Its hanging folds covered the holster he had to have down his right leg, unless he was wearing that low-slung cartridge belt just to keep folks from calling him a sissy. He needed a shave, and the watery blue eyes staring out sort of crawfishlike from under the battered brim of his sun-faded tan Carlsbad made the hair tingle on the nape of Longarm's neck. That was before the normally jovial but now somewhat ashen-faced newspaper man explained in as jovial a tone as he could manage, "This young gent would be Deputy Sheriff Fulton Steele from Boulder County, Your Honor. He and his sidekick are down here looking to get the views of Longarm on that post office robbery up near Jamestown a spell back."

Steele, if that was his name, pressed closer to the heavy-set Crawford, growling, "I told you I was here alone, should anyone ask."

The newspaper man smiled fondly at him and replied, "Hell, anyone can see that. I only meant to tell the judge here you were in town on serious business with your posse or whatever, see?"

Longarm was starting to see, whether anyone else might or not. The one calling himself Steele was covering Crawford with his sixgun, under that tan duster. Thanks to Crawford's "slip" Longarm knew there were at least two of them laying for him in there. He knew they had to be laying for him because of the slick way Crawford had introduced him as the much older and much better-dressed Judge Dickerson. Crawford had hoped, correctly, that anyone in a suit and shoestring tie who didn't desperately need a shave and a haircut would strike such a saddle tramp as more dignified.

In the meanwhile it seemed obvious Longarm was supposed to say something. So he tried. "As a matter of fact, I was just talking to Longarm across the way. I asked him if he'd like to come over here and help me polish off the pigs' feet. But he said something about his boss, Marshal Vail, sending him out to Aurora this afternoon."

It was too early to tell whether it had worked or not. The gunslick holding that gun on Crawford seemed undecided whether to piss his pants or bust out crying as he protested, half to himself, "That's not the way things was supposed to go this afternoon. They told us Longarm comes here most every lunch hour, to order his fool self a needled beer and drift down to this end of the bar to stuff his fool face."

"They told you true," said Crawford, more lightly than he must have felt. "You can always tell when Longarm's been by because there's not a boiled egg or a pig's foot to be seen once he's grazed through here. Isn't that right, Judge?"

Longarm smiled thinly and reached for a little sissy ham-on-rye as he replied in a desperately casual tone, "That's true. I hate pigs' feet myself. I think he said something about eating in Aurora, once he finished his chore out yonder."

The lunch hour crowd in the taproom on the far side of Crawford and the proddy-eyed Steele was starting to thin a bit, but not nearly as much as Longarm preferred for his innocent bystanders when and if a firefight should commence. There was no way to ask Crawford which of the doors behind him figured to pop open in the event things got even tenser around there. It stood to reason the other gunman was holed up to one side of the passage or the other. Then that pretty but spoken-for redhead who'd gotten him in trouble with Miss Morgana out at the orphan asylum came down the far side of the bar with a tray of fresh cold cuts to see if she could get him killed.

The perky redhead didn't know what she was doing, bless her, when she favored Longarm with a sunny smile and said, "Howdy, Custis. I didn't see you come in. I fear we're running low on pigs' feet, but here's some of that head cheese you like."

Longarm tensed, wondering how in thunder he and Crawford were both supposed to come out alive. But as the redhead put the tray down and turned away, the gunslick laying for Deputy U.S. Marshal Custis Long simply licked his lips and muttered, "I don't like this. They told us Longarm's usually early at this here free-lunch counter!"

Longarm couldn't meet Crawford's relieved eyes. Knowing Steele was uninformed as to his full name as well as exact description, Longarm took a modest bite of ham-on-rye, wishing he had beer to wash it down but not about to call that redhead back, and tried, "I just told you the ugly cuss wasn't coming. You know where Aurora is, don't you?"

Steele looked too miserable for a rider who knew the way to the next trail stop east, across some open prairie Longarm could hardly wait to spy such a bozo on, alone or in modest numbers. So Longarm said, "Hell, you can walk to Aurora from here if it's important. Might be somewhat faster if you took the Colfax Street car line halfways, or better yet, had a pony under you for say an hour or more. You didn't walk down here from Boulder County, did you?"

Steele swore softly, half to himself, then he suddenly blurted, "Hey, Raymond? You'd best come out here and talk to these birds. That Longarm the professor sent us to meet has gone off to some infernal town calt Aurora!"

There was no answer for a moment. Steele called, more plaintively, "Raymond?" Then one of the doors of one of those private rooms popped open and a stockier but just as rustic-looking individual grumped out, replying, "Jesus H.

31

Christ, can't you follow directions better than that, Fulton? What's going on out here anyways?"

Longarm had to worry about that gun muzzle pressed against poor Crawford's floating rib before he worried about anything else, so he made a deliberately awkward feint with his gun hand and, as he'd hoped, both greener gunslicks threw down on him at once. So after that, things went much more predictably.

Knowing the one with his gun already out, although hidden by that duster, was the more dangerous target, Longarm simply shot Steele in the heart, point blank, the moment Steele swung his gun muzzle away from the newspaper man's side.

At the same time he shot Steele with the derringer palmed in his left hand, Longarm sprang backwards so that he was no longer there when the second one, Raymond, drew and fired in one smooth motion.

Then Longarm had whipped his own .44—40 out of its cross-draw holster to fire even smoother and send Raymond staggering back into the private room he'd just vacated. As the gunslick crashed to the floor in there, Longarm snapped, "Cover Steele, Crawford!" and tore through his own gunsmoke, firing blind in case anyone was still up inside. But once he'd rejoined old Raymond in there, he saw the round he'd put in the rascal's rib cage had just about finished him off. As he stood over the dying Raymond, reloading his sixgun with the derringer just cooling in a side pocket for now, Longarm told his victim, "I hate to be the one who has to tell you this, Raymond. But I ain't exactly Federal Judge Dickerson and you ain't exactly an assassin worthy of the name neither."

"You're a friend of Longarm's, eh?" the gent bleeding into the sawdust at his feet replied bleary-eyed.

Crawford came in to join them, softly saying, "Some of the regulars have gone for the Denver P.D. Thanks, pard. I thought I was a gone goose when that other one shoved his gun in my ribs, evoking your name in vain."

Longarm asked who was covering young Steele. Crawford said, "The management, with more sawdust and a tarp, for now. When you shoot a man you don't fuck around, do you?"

Longarm shrugged and hunkered down beside the one called Raymond, his reloaded sixgun still out but aimed more politely as he told the profusely bleeding rascal, "It's my considered opinion I just killed you too, Raymond. I never meant it personal, and I'll be proud to see both you boys are buried in separate boxes, with your names sand-blasted on patent markers, if you'd like to clarify just a few details for me and the *Denver Post* here."

Raymond said, "Go to hell. You was Longarm all the time, right?"

To which Longarm could only modestly reply, "Yep. The professor told you I'd be by for the free lunch around noon. He just neglected to tell you how in thunder you were supposed to single me out from all the other tall, dark, and handsome strangers who frequent these premises."

Raymond grumbled, "Fulton wasn't supposed to act like such an asshole. Did you hull him good, I hope?"

Longarm nodded soberly and said, "I got you too, Raymond. So how's about telling us what you'd like on your grave marker and who you'd like us to invite to your funeral? You'll want your pal, the professor, to say a few words over you, won't you?"

Raymond's voice sounded far away and sort of tinny as he blinked his eyelids rapidly and replied, "I doubt he'll want to come, being he's such a famous outlaw and . . . Hey, how come it's so dark in here now?"

Longarm shook the dying gunslick's shoulder and insisted, "Tell us how to get in touch with Jethro Markham, Raymond. We know he's not at the old Paget soddy. Where do you take recruits from there? Somewhere closer to Boulder?"

The dying gunslick muttered something about that old cabin on the South Saint Vrain, and then he died.

So Longarm muttered, "Shit," and shut his eyelids for him.

Crawford said, "The South Saint Vrain's a white-water mountain stream up in Boulder County, isn't it?"

Longarm nodded soberly and replied, "Runs through the mountain town of Lyons. So does a spur of the Chicago, Burlington, and Quincy Railroad. That soddy they were using yesterday in Adams County was just outside a modest town with railroad connections, and the hills around Lyons are infested with abandoned cabins. You say Steele told you he rode official for Boulder County?"

The reporter reached for his notebook as he nodded and explained, "They both claimed to be deputy sheriffs. Their conversation commenced a lot friendlier than it was going by the time you showed up, bless your unusual approach to free eats. Someone must have pointed me out to them as a regular who knew you on sight. They fed me some bull about being fellow lawmen who wanted to talk to you, and then, when I asked to see some I.D., things started to get sort of ugly."

Longarm had found Raymond's wallet by this time. The dead man had known more about pickpockets than serious gunfighting, apparently. As Longarm drew the billfold from its sneaky pocket in the otherwise ordinary denim jacket, it felt sort of fat for the modest costume of its owner. Longarm unfolded it and muttered, "What the fuck?" as he found himself face-to-face with a deputy sheriff's pewter badge that looked disturbingly authentic.

He'd just speculated aloud on this when Billy Vail grumped in from the main taproom, growling, "Now you've done it, old son, unless you've a mighty good story to go with gunning that Boulder County deputy outside and . . . Jesus H. Christ, who's that one, you murderous young cuss?"

Reporter Crawford replied for both of them, saying, "Another deputy of the same sheriff, from the looks of things, Marshal Vail. My paper will be proud to print the

34

story and, as you'll see, Longarm only did what he had to. The one out front had a sixgun jabbed in my ribs, and that one there was holed up in here with the announced intent of dealing with Longarm just as Longarm dealt with him instead."

Vail stared soberly down at the body sprawled at their feet as he grudgingly decided, "All right, anyone loco enough to go gunning for Longarm in his own neighborhood saloon would likely be loco enough to beg, borrow, or steal some novelty-shop badges."

But Longarm shook his head as he handed the billfold he'd had time to examine to Vail, saying, "This badge looks real. The sheriff's department I.D. made out to one Raymond Wade has the officious seal of Boulder County stamped on her as well."

Vail held the incriminating evidence up to the light, exclaiming, "Well, I never! Why in thunder would real lawmen set out to gun an innocent soul like you, old son?"

Longarm put away his sixgun and got out the derringer to reload. "Works more ways than one, Boss. Raymond Wade here sounds as if he could have been kin to the Lem and Rafe Wade killed out at the Paget soddy yesterday. Had old Raymond asked me, I could have assured him I shot neither of the ugly mutts. But since I'm better known than most of the lawmen who were out there, and since even some half-ass lawmen hold with an eye for an eye and a tooth for a tooth—"

"That works," Vail cut in. "It wouldn't be the first time the same family's had members riding on both sides of the law, or the first time a hothead packing a badge lost track of which side he was supposed to be riding for."

Reporter Crawford, who'd covered more than one such dismal event in his own time, said, "Hold on, Marshal. What about young Steele out there?"

Vail said Sergeant Nolan of the Denver P.D. was watching that stiff until the meat wagon arrived.

Longarm put his reloaded derringer back in his vest pocket

and said, "What Crawford means is that Steele seemed to be taking any feud I might have with the Wades at least as seriously, and just now, as he was checking out, old Raymond allowed that both of 'em had been sent after me by guess who!"

Crawford saved Vail the trouble by saying, "Some Professor Jethro, and wasn't there something about a new hideout on the South Saint Vrain, Longarm?"

It was Vail who replied with a snort of disbelief. "Aw, come on! First you want me to buy at least some of the staff at Iowa State Prison aiding and abetting the escape of a convicted lifer, and next you want me to buy two Colorado lawmen corrupted by the same fool crook? How would your professor go about all that, old son?"

Longarm shrugged and said, "For openers, I'd hardly call anyone that slick a fool. But as you pointed out earlier, neither escaping from a state prison nor setting up some sort of school for wayward youths comes under federal jurisdiction, right?"

It worked. Vail grabbed Longarm by one arm and proceeded to haul him outside, growling, "I'll be the judge of who's allowed to do what along the South Saint Vrain—which, as I recall, runs for many a mountain mile through federal open range. But let's talk about it back at the office. We got us some planning to do that I'd just as soon not read about in the *Denver Post* until I'm good and ready."

Crawford of the *Post* just smiled. But Longarm protested, "Hold on, now, Billy. I ain't ready to go back to the office yet. Thanks to what just transpired here, I never got my beer and free lunch."

Vail said, "Tough shit. It was your grand notion and none of my own to get into a shootout instead of the free lunch just now."

Chapter 4

It was possible, albeit mighty complicated, to ride all the way up to Lyons from Denver by rail. Longarm boarded the afternoon local for Boulder City instead. He had more than one good reason. He was going to need at least two ponies once he began to explore the range around Lyons in any case. So it would be almost as fast, and doubtless far more surprising to the professor and his pupils, if he just hired some riding and packing stock at the county seat and sort of eased into Lyons by way of the woodlot out back. The two towns lay separated by ten or twelve miles of timbered ridges and cow-cluttered grassy glens, where it wasn't fenced private.

Commencing his discreet approach from the county seat had some other advantages to a federal lawman on tolerable terms with at least some of the gents on the county board of supervisors. It seemed doubtful the sheriff himself knew anything about his wayward deputies Wade and Steele yet, if they had really been working for Boulder County to begin with. Until he had that loose end trimmed, he meant to play his cards closer to the vest than usual and to hell with courtesy calls he was supposed to pay on local lawmen.

Last but not least, Longarm was hungry as a bitch wolf by the time he, Billy Vail, and that damned slow typist Henry had his mission authorized on paper, if not too clear in anyone's head.

The slow-moving local didn't rate a club car, and the stale sandwiches the candy butcher sold him with a bottle of orange soda pop had doubtless been intended as field rations for the Union Army when they'd first been wrapped in wax paper, shortly after the first battle of Bull Run. The orange pop helped. It was wet enough to wash the stale bread down and awful enough to ruin his appetite before he was halfway done. The bitty snot-nosed Indian kid in the seat ahead of him was sort of unappetizing too. The kid was about three, a disgusting age for kids of any race, and his Indian mamma seated with her back to Longarm didn't seem to care, or notice, the way her brat was drooling over the back of their seat.

On second glance, the little Arapaho, if he wasn't Ute, seemed much more interested in the white man's uneaten ham-and-Swiss-on-rye than in anyone's scalp. So Longarm held the stale sandwich out to the bitty Indian, to see it snatched from his fingers by one tiny brown fist and devoured in a rapid-fire series of pack-rat bites that could only mean pure and simple starvation. The kid put away the whole stale sandwich, and was whimpering for more when the Indian woman sitting next to him popped back from wherever she'd been drifting to ask him something in her own soft liquid lingo. Longarm recognized the sound of her "Ho" or Ute-Shoshone dialect better than he followed her drift. But he was able to figure she was asking the kid what in thunder he had in his fool mouth now, and cleared his own throat to awkwardly call out, "If you savvy my lingo, ma'am, I just let your boy polish off the last of a sandwich with me. I got some soda pop here, if you think he can manage it without winding up all sticky."

The Indian gal turned all the way round in her seat to stare sort of hollow-eyed at Longarm. She was dressed shabby-white, save for the Shoshone headband holding her parted and braided black hair in place. She'd have been prettier, for an Indian gal, if she hadn't looked so malnourished and careworn. She answered him in her own tongue. Longarm knew that a sort of plaintive crow-caw meant "no," and that what sounded like "salt wattle" likely meant "white man's water," which was close enough to soda pop when you thought about it. So he just nodded and withdrew his offer while the thirsty little kid followed every motion of the pop bottle with his big wistful eyes.

Having settled the matter to suit her proud fancy, the Indian gal turned her back on Longarm to stare stiffly out at the passing scenery, dull as it was. Denver only looked as if it lay smack against the Front Range of the Rockies from, say, a hotel window. The town of Boulder was much closer, and you really could traipse up a Rocky Mountain from most any hotel in Boulder without wearing your fool self out. So the tracks got to wind through the short-grass-covered hogbacks where the High Plains met the Front Range, and as they got ever closer to Boulder, it commenced to get more obvious why they'd named the place so unimaginatively.

There were mighty few Sioux in Sioux City, and hardly a saint worth mention in Saint Lou or Saint Joe. But there were more blamed boulders in the vicinity of Boulder, Colorado, than one would think the Lord had ever needed in those mere seven days of Creation. Granite outcrops bursting through the rolling range all about made Longarm think of petrified thunderheads, or maybe mighty piles of dead and bloated elephants. There were patches of timber sprouting on every third or fourth rise now, as the tracks took them up the gentle but considerable grade. He knew there'd been much more timber in the foothills back in what the Indians wistfully called "The Shining Times." But if there was one thing mining men, cattle men, and sodbuster men agreed on, it seemed to be that trees got in the way of progress and were meant for pit-props, fence posts, or firewood.

The young candy butcher was coming along the aisle again, anxious to make some last sales to greenhorns who might not know they were almost there now. So thinking about wistful Indians, Longarm waved the kid over and said he'd buy a chocolate bar if the candy butcher would get rid of this pop bottle for him. The candy butcher grinned and took the half-filled bottle, saying chocolate sold for a nickel a bar on that line.

Longarm bought one anyway, and as the rapacious young cuss moved on and the Indian kid watched, big-eyed, Longarm soberly unwrapped lead foil from the modest slab of milk chocolate and handed it to the hungry-looking little shit, putting a finger to his own lips in hopes of keeping their negotiations a secret.

He hoped in vain. The kid was so delighted with the tasty trifle that his mother noticed before he'd put away half of it. She was too smart to slap milk chocolate away from a starving child, but she still sounded mad as a wet hen as she exclaimed, "He no need. Me no want. We got own people meeting us in Boulder. So you no fuck this person, Saltu prick!"

Longarm chuckled indulgently and replied, "Perish the thought, ma'am. I only shared some grub and sweets with your boy to keep from wasting it. Anyone can see you're both gentlefolk, of the Ho persuasion leastways."

Her eyes widened and she began to natter at him in pure Shoshone. He laughed sheepishly and replied, "Hold on, ma'am. I know you folk call yourselves Ho and refer to my kind as Saltu. After that your, ah, Saltu has my Ho beat pitiful. But let's not worry about it, seeing as we don't really have nothing to argue about."

She stared soberly at him and tried in her own awkward English. "Me said I think you must be good person. You no get mad, like other Saltu, when I say I no fuck, even for present."

Then she frowned thoughtfully and added, "Maybe you think Winkatli not fuck good as Saltu woman?"

The car they were in wasn't all that crowded, but they didn't have it entirely to themselves either. So he leaned forward to softly murmur, "I'm sure you're a swell fuck, Miss Winkatli. But let's not talk about it no more. We'll be rolling into Boulder any minute and we sure don't want folk spreading gossip about us in such a small town."

He doubted she knew what he was talking about but, as in the case of soothing words to spooked livestock, his tone got her to simmer down. She warned him not to follow her and the boy too closely as they all got off at Boulder. Then she turned her back on him some more and just let him guess why. He didn't strain his brain too hard. He knew he'd stare thoughtfully at any strange cuss buttering up to a sort of pretty kinswoman getting off a train if he'd been expecting her to get off unescorted.

The train began to slow and the scenery outside commenced to get more interesting before the awkward silence had lasted long enough to hurt. Knowing the train would be rolling on for Greeley and Fort Collins, once it had jerked boiler water in Boulder, Longarm rose to his considerable height to mosey forward, towards the baggage car. He'd naturally stowed his McClellan, Winchester, and other heavier possibles up forward, and not even a jealous husband of the Shoshone persuasion could find fault with a man he'd never seen before getting out of a different car entirely from his pretty wife and ugly kid.

As he stood on the open platform, pounding on the rear door of the baggage car, a railroad crewman he knew opened the door a crack to tell him he couldn't come in between stations. Then he saw who it was, and let him in, saying, "Heard you was aboard, Longarm. What's up? You ain't really expecting 'em to stop this local in broad-ass daylight, are you?"

Longarm shook his head and said, "I got a saddle and some other gear up here somewheres. I'm sorry you heard I was aboard this train. I boarded a slow string of day coaches at the last minute with more privacy than that in mind. But I reckon that's the trouble with passing through downtown Denver, once you've been written up in both the *Post* and the *News*."

The crewman in charge of the baggage car agreed that was about the size of it and led the way forward where, sure enough, Longarm's old army saddle with his rifle, saddlebags, and bedroll lashed to it had been perched atop a mahogany coffin with gold-plated trim and handles. Nobody who'd been through the slaughter at Shiloh would really blanch. But the crew member noted the thoughtful look in Longarm's eyes and said, "The cadaver in the box never died of nothing catching, and they got plenty of formalin in him as well as plenty of charcoal under him. Young feller got his fool self shot in a brush with some Indian Police, down near Denver. It's a shame he did. Hailed from a fine old Boulder County family, but you know how some kids are when it comes to wild oats."

Longarm scowled at the mysterious coffin, muttering, half to himself, "I'm missing something here. I know for a fact that a couple of Boulder County boys went down in the Parthenon Saloon this very day. But neither body would have been released by the coroner's office yet. Could I see the manifest as goes with this particular freight, Mike?"

The crewman nodded but said, "Save us some time if you was to say just what it was you wanted to know, Longarm. I just told you we're running a dead man up to Boulders so's his kin can plant him in their family plot."

Longarm asked the family name. Things got even less clear when the man who was supposed to know said, "Farnsworth. Rafe Farnsworth, Junior, as a matter of fact. The only son of Major Raphael Farnsworth of the Third Colorado. That was during the war, of course. Since he mostly fought Cheyenne for the Union, the major's been raising beef up around Trapper's Rock."

Longarm scowled at the fancy coffin under his own saddle and said, in a bemused tone, "I know where Trapper's Rock is, and now that you mention it, I've heard of the big Rocking F outfit you have to be jawing about. The question before the house is, who in thunder could be in that damned box!"

Mike said, "I just told you."

But Longarm shook his head and said, "I was there when the Cherokee Police accounted for exactly four young owlhoot riders. No more. No less. Bart Larkin was taken alive. His kid brother, Festus, was taken alive but badly wounded. The other two, Lem and Rafe Wade, were killed. Earlier today I shot it out with Raymond Wade and Fulton Steele. Nobody else in Denver has shot it out with any damned body in recent memory. So how in blue blazes did we wind up with a gunshot victim called Farnsworth unless . . . "

"Raphael ain't a common name, unless you're an archangel," the helpful crew member pointed out.

Longarm started to object. Then he nodded soberly and said, "A man who'd lie about his last name could just as easily call an asshole pal his brother. Billy the Kid says his name's really William Bonney and that he went bad defending the honor of his widowed mother."

"Ain't that so?" asked Mike, who read Ned Buntline's magazine now and again.

Longarm grimaced and said, "Not hardly. The surly little shit they call Billy the Kid was born Henry McCarthy on the east side of New York City. His father died when he was little. The widow McCarthy married up with a fairly decent cuss called William Antrim and they all moved west to Silver City, New Mexico Territory, where the kid went bad."

Mike nodded and said, "Right, he stabbed a man who'd insulted his poor widowed mamma and . . . Hold on, what was the man of the house doing whilst all this was going on?"

Longarm shrugged and said, "Working his usual shift in

43

the silver mine, I reckon. Mrs. Antrim ran a boardinghouse. The kid should have been working himself, but he took to stealing instead. He never killed anyone in Silver City for any reason. He was charged with stealing some fancy laundry and just never showed up for his hearing after they'd let his folks take him home. He might have killed his first man, a colored blacksmith, in Camp Bowie a few years later. But to hell with an outlaw I ain't after, not this season. How do we go about opening this coffin, Mike?"

The railroader looked stricken and protested, "We don't! I'd as soon let you open the safe down to the far end of this car if I wanted to lose my job that desperate. They might hold an open casket ceremony up near Trapper's Rock, Lord willing and they get him up there soon enough in this weather."

Longarm looked undecided. Mike went on. "Nights are still cool and the days haven't really started heating up, in the hills, this early. There'd be pure hell to pay if we was to deliver that fine mahogany coffin all messed up with crowbar and hammer marks."

Longarm reached a decision. "Well, Trapper's Rock ain't really too far out of my way, once I mount up to follow the trail to Lyons anyway. But I sure am commencing to feel confused about who in thunder's supposed to be in which coffin."

Mike found that even more confusing. So Longarm tersely brought the friendly railroader up to date and Mike agreed. "It reminds me of them shell games my daddy always warned me never to take part in. But don't it stand to reason a professor who got 'em to plant another convict in his stead would teach his crooked pupils never to give their right names as they rid around robbing folk?"

The train was moving at no more than a crawl now. Longarm lifted his saddle and other baggage from the mysterious coffin and replied that he'd just said as much. Mike slid the side door open as the train braked to a complete stop, hissing like a weary sidewinder. It only took Longarm a few seconds to get his bearings and drop to the planking of the platform. The shingle-covered depot and the street beyond were to his left. So that was the way he headed with a view to wiring Billy Vail he'd arrived and hiring himself those two ponies before he did anything else.

Under less unusual conditions Longarm would have wanted to scout up a hotel room instead this late in the day. The sun was low above the purple ridges to the west, and he knew at least the brighter stars would be winking down from the east by the time he could ride far enough out of town to matter. But he wasn't about to drift into Lyons discreetly if he kept letting folk along the way get a good gander at him.

He hoped that by camping out along the trail without a night fire he might confuse others half as much as they were confusing him. The idea was to get the hell off this railroad property and drop out of sight before everyone in Boulder noticed he was up this way.

Suiting his actions to his aspirations, Longarm forged on through the waiting room where, sure enough, a modest war band of Shoshone dressed in Indian Agency duds had gathered to greet that pretty young mother and her ugly little boy. He didn't look back to see how far behind him along the platform they might be. He went on across the fresh-tarred road to the Western Union office, one stirrup of his McClellan kicking him in the shins all the way, and toted his load inside to plant it atop the counter, pick up a stub pencil, and get off a terse message to Billy Vail. He told the clerk to send it to Denver at night-letter rates, and when the Western Union man pointed out how short it was, he insisted, "Bill us off-hour rates anyways. My boss is so worried about that nickel a word you charge for straight wires that you'd think it was his own money instead of the taxpayers'."

The clerk said, wistfully, that he wished they'd let him vote for at least one public official like that, but concluded, on a brighter note, "It could be worse. Did you know Queen

Victoria's made that cruel Income Tax of 1874 permanent as well as compulsive?"

Longarm said, "Jesus H. Christ, we got rid of the British Crown and its peculiar notions just in time, didn't we?" Then he picked up his saddle and gear to tote outside in the soft light of a Rocky Mountain sunset.

He'd used the same livery more than once up this way, so that was the way he was heading along the plank walk when a shrill female voice wailed, "Saltu! Duck!"

So Longarm dove headfirst, with the saddle ahead of him, into the narrow space between the plank walk and a watering trough fashioned of the same sun-silvered material. He sensed he'd done the right thing, despite some earlier reservations, when a not-too-distant rifle spanged three bullets into the thin planking of the trough to water his hat with three pissy streams and inspire him to get his sixgun out *poco tiempo*.

He knew that was a rifle lobbing lead at him, likely a Henry lever action, because of its rate of fire. He knew his Colt .44−40 fired faster, making up for its shorter range, as close-in as this silly son of a bitch seemed to be. But when he'd rolled away from his upside-down McClellan to pop up armed and dangerous a good eight or ten feet from that watering trough, there was nothing to be seen more dangerous than a drifting cloud of gunsmoke near the corner of the hat shop up from the Western Union office.

Across the way, in front of the depot, that Indian gal with the chocolate-smeared kid was pointing due north and yelling in her own lingo at him. Longarm didn't need a Ho dictionary to savvy she was saying something like, "They went thataway."

But he owed her and her stolid-looking kin more than a wave in return. So he went back, picked up his stuff, and headed back over with the McClellan up on one shoulder as he kept his gun out, polite, in his right fist.

As he headed for the Shoshone, smiling, a little skinny runt wearing a silvery beard and badge to match came tear-

46

ing down the walk on that side, his own gun out, to demand, "Who fired them shots just now and how come you got a gun trained on them redskins, mister?"

Longarm swore softly under his breath and called back, "It ain't them I'm sore at, ah, Constable. A timely Indian whoop just saved my bacon as a matter of fact, and so much for slipping in and out of Boulder without attracting any infernal notice!"

One Indian, dressed like a cowboy, whoever he was related to, spoke tolerable English. So he got to explain things to the town law while Longarm listened, just as interested. For he'd never seen the rifle-toting back-shooter at all, and didn't see how he'd have ever seen much of anything again if that Indian gal hadn't yelled so good.

From where they'd been jawing about transportation in front of the depot the Indians had all gotten at least a glimpse of Longarm's would-be assassin. After that opinions varied as to what the Saltu might have looked like. The general impression Longarm was left with was a tall or short white man wearing shotgun chaps or jeans and a buckskin or maybe denim jacket. They all agreed he'd been packing a lever-action carbine and that he'd lit out to the north between the hat shop and hardware store next door, once he'd noticed his intended target was still alive and doubtless fixing to start shooting back at any time.

By the time they had all this sorted out, they'd been joined by two more lawmen and at least two dozen curious townsmen. One of the lawmen who'd drifted over was sporting the same county badge the late Raymond Wade had been packing down in Denver. But when Longarm casually asked if anyone around there knew Deputy Wade, nobody seemed to. The town law said, "Well, seeing nobody seems to have been hurt and seeing it's past my supper time, I'm writing this off as boisterous behavior on the part of a party or parties unknown, unless I hear any objections."

He didn't. Longarm was no fool, and nobody else there

had a wet hat. Pausing only long enough to thank the Indians again, Longarm lugged his awkward load after that one deputy with the county badge, who noticed. As the man broke stride and fixed him with a curious smile, Longarm said, "I forgot to tell you that Boulder deputy called Wade is cooling off in the Denver Morgue right now. We got another stiff called Fulton Steele. Both of 'em claimed to ride for your outfit and had the badges and I.D. to prove it. Your turn, pard."

The deputy he'd just caught up with shook his head and seemed calm enough as he answered, "Never heard of neither. Of course, his nibs will hand out honorary badges, being a politician first and a lawman once he gets reelected this fall. I'd have heard them names before if either rid with us regular, though. We ain't got more than a company of deputies in the whole county and I've ridden with most every one of 'em in my time."

Longarm thought before he decided. "Those badges looked real, but then an honorary badge would, wouldn't it? The printed credentials may have been what they were worried about. One of 'em pulled his gun on a Denver boy who wanted a closer look and . . . Yep, that works. It would say something like Honorary or Just Funning on anything your sheriff passed out as a play-pretty, right?"

The real county rider shrugged and said he wouldn't know, since it wasn't his job to get out the vote. Longarm asked, "Who do I want to see about it then? This being the county seat where all such records ought to be kept."

The helpful but likely hungry county rider shot a wistful glance at the orange and purple sky above as he replied, "Nobody, at this hour. You might want to check at the sheriff's office or county clerk's in the morning. You'll find both in the basement of the county courthouse, back up the other way. I don't know where you think you're headed but I'm headed home for supper, and no offense, my old woman can get sort of shrill when I bring strangers home for supper without letting her know at least a day ahead."

48

Longarm chuckled, said that was one reason he was still single, and then they parted friendly. Longarm turned back the way they'd just come, not to pay a call on a courthouse closed for the night, but because the only decent hotel he knew of in town was back that way as well.

On the way he passed the livery and so, while he decided on a new strategy, with the cat out of the bag and some new sign to follow, he lugged his clumsy saddle and heavy gear inside to bet the old geezer in charge a quarter that they wouldn't let him use their tack room before he was ready to hire a couple of ponies from them.

He lost, as he'd hoped he might, but hung on to the Winchester from his saddle boot as he continued on to the hotel with a springier step and both eyes peeled for sudden movement in the gathering dusk.

Since it was obvious friend and foe alike knew he was in town, and since he meant to bed down all alone upstairs, Longarm registered under his real name and hired a corner room with cross ventilation. When he asked about indoor plumbing the snot-nosed desk clerk, who reminded him of Henry back in Denver, told him there was a chamber pot under the bed and that if that wasn't fancy enough for him, he ought to go back to the big city, where they had time to mess with such fastidious folk. So Longarm allowed he'd just piss in the desk clerk's ear if he didn't watch his big mouth, and after that they seemed to get along tolerable.

He asked if there was any place in those parts where a man could get a decent bowl of chili con carne. The desk clerk suggested a hole-in-the-wall just a few doors down. So Longarm took the Winchester up to his hired room and, lighting the small bed lamp, made sure there really was a chamber pot and that nobody had used it recently. The bed linens seemed fresh as well, even though they were in fact cotton muslin under a quilted counterpane of more colors than Joseph's coat in the Good Book.

Bracing the carbine in a corner by the head of the bed, Longarm blew out the bed lamp again and stepped out

49

into the gloomy second-story corridor. Unless they meant to light that hanging lamp down by the one window, it figured to be black as a bitch up there ere long. For the only illumination was that provided through the window, free, by the last purple light of the gloaming.

As long as he had the gloomy corridor all to himself, Longarm hunkered down with his door still ajar to thrust the stem of the match he'd just used into the crack just below the bottom hinge. Then he shoved the door all the way shut, rose, and made sure it was locked before he pocketed the key and went downstairs to investigate that chili joint.

He found it where the clerk had told him to look for it. He knew at first sniff that the fat old gal behind the counter was really Mex and not say Arapaho or Shoshone, moon-faced and sloe-eyed as she might be. When he ordered in his own version of Spanish she seemed delighted, and confided in the same lingo that a lot of Anglos up this way seemed to take her for Indio, for some reason. He chuckled fondly and replied, "Well, that circle skirt you got on under your apron does look Indian, even if we both know it's a Chihuahua Indian design. But to tell the truth I knew you couldn't be Indio as soon as I smelled that chili in the pot, or those tortillas I suspect you only made this very day."

So she told him he was on the money, and it was a good thing he ordered plenty of tortillas to go with his *chili con carne y cerveza*. For even with beer on the side, he had to take a chaw of bland cornmeal tortilla with every bite or so of her ferocious chili to keep from moaning out loud.

By the time she served him a slab of *pastelillo de man-zanas* and *cafe negro* strong enough to clean guns with, they were flirting sort of sassy, if only for practice on his part. He was sort of tempted to take her up on it, knowing a woman who cooked that swell was doubtless anxious to please men, and knowing that that was more important, once the lights were out, than what a gal might look like with all her duds on by the cruel true light of day. But even if she was as willing as she was acting, and even if that snot-nosed desk clerk would let him entertain a guest so dark after dark, he suspected he'd regret it, whether the poor fat thing got caught in any cross fire or not before it came time to ride on.

So, quitting while he was ahead and tipping her a whole quarter to show he hadn't been just mocking her, Longarm settled for a toothpick instead of a feel and ambled back toward his hotel.

It was way too early for anyone but chickens and children to be seriously thinking of sleep. But for the same reasons he'd just passed on a lady who sure liked things hot, he decided to avoid such bright lights and piano-tinkles as the one main street had to offer after dark. It was way harder to back-shoot a man in bed behind a locked door than standing at a bar with his back to a roomful of strangers, and so far he didn't even know whether that asshole with the Henry had been wearing a white hat or a black hat.

Knowing his own sleeping habits and distaste for counting sheep, Longarm stopped at a corner cigar store to stock up on more cheroots and the latest edition of the *Denver Post,* all just in by mail train, according to the shopkeeper. The first cheroot Longarm lit, outside, tasted a mite stale. But that wasn't saying the old bird was a liar. Tobacco dried out fast and funny-tasting at this altitude.

Back at the hotel, the desk clerk seemed to be taking a leak or jerking off somewhere in the back. Longarm didn't care. He'd long since learned not to leave his fool key at the desk when he went out. It only meant you had to pick it up when you came in and, no matter what the hotel regulations might say, Longarm knew that as long as a guest was paid up in advance, the help would just as soon have him let himself in and out without pestering them.

The stairs creaked a mite, going up them, until he moved closer to one wall where they didn't. He did this without thinking, the way he checked his guns and pocket watch

51

every morning before starting the day. A man in his line of work didn't need exact reasons for avoiding empty gun chambers and clumsy footsteps. If he waited for real emergencies to behave like a pro, he wasn't a pro.

Upstairs, he found someone had lit that one hall lamp after all. It was sort of hard to tell. It was a thundering wonder how they got that lamp wick to burn at all, trimmed that low. The feeble light it shed was more blue than anything else. It barely cast a shadow on the threadbare rug ahead of him as he strode on to his corner room. But when he got there he still had enough light to see that match stem winking up at him from between the baseboard and hall runner, where he'd never put it to begin with.

First moves coming first, Longarm drew his .44–40 with his right hand and got rid of the cheroot he'd been smoking with the left. Once he'd planted the smoke in the spittoon nearest his door at that end of the dark corridor, he was stuck with the harder parts. So he took a deep breath, grasped the brass knob firmly with his left hand, and when he found the door unlocked, swung it open fast and moved in even faster in a pantherlike crouch.

The dark figure lying in wait on the other side gave a strangled gasp of surprise and fired blind where Longarm's chest might have been if he'd just come through that door like an innocent total asshole. Then Longarm had grabbed the hot barrel of his visitor's carbine with his left hand and swept the space where someone's damned head should have been with a vicious back-handed whip with his gun hand, gun and all. But his opponent was way shorter than expected and all Longarm hit with his pistol barrel was the empty crown of a taller hat and the wallpaper behind him, next to the door. But by then, of course, he'd let go of the carbine to throw a hard left hook with that empty hand, and this time his punch landed solidly, to send the much smaller intruder across the bed and into a far corner to just sprawl there, limp as a rag doll, for now.

So Longarm had the bed lamp lit and his visitor's long

gun kicked under the bed by the time someone pounded on the door to call out, "What's going on up here? We don't allow no shooting in this hotel, dad blast it!"

Longarm called back, calmer than he really felt, "Don't shoot nothing off then. That wasn't me just now."

The desk clerk, house dick, or whatever insisted, "I smell fresh gunsmoke out here, cowboy!"

To which Longarm replied, "I don't see why you're pestering me in here about it then. I'm not a cowboy. I'm the law. Federal. And I'd sure take it kindly if you'd let me get back to what I was doing in here before some damn fool commenced to wake the dead out there."

The curious cuss outside went off to pound on some other doors. By this time the stranger he'd knocked galley west was starting to moan softly from the floor on the far side of the bed. So Longarm circled around the foot of the bed, his revolver still in hand, to softly call out, "I'm coming, Short Stuff. As you might have just surmised, I wanted you all to myself, and now we're going to have us some man-to-man talk unless you'd like a kick in the nuts to refresh your memory."

Then he saw who and what he'd just decked with a left hook and continued, "Oh, sorry, ma'am. I take back what I just said about kicking you in the nuts, but you'd still better answer me some questions *poco tiempo,* if you don't want to go from here direct to the female cell block of the nearest available jailhouse!"

The slim athletic-looking brunette in the mannish blue denim jeans and jacket sat up straighter, bracing her upper body in the corner as she wiped her lush lips with the back of one suntanned wrist, and said, "You cut my lip, you son of a bitch!" She calmly reached for her overturned black Stetson to put it back on, adding, "All right, you've got the edge on me for now, you brute, but sooner or later I'll kill you and you have my word on that!"

Longarm saw she wasn't wearing a gun rig around her slender denim-clad hips. So he held his own gun polite as he

53

sat on the bed just above her drawn-up and Justin-booted feet before he asked, pleasantly enough, "How come, ma'am? I'd have never hit you so hard, just now, had I known you were a member of the unfair sex. I wouldn't have hit you anyway, if you hadn't been laying for me in here with that Henry .44 and an obvious intent to blow my poor head off!"

She drew her knees higher and wiped her split lip again, saying, "Don't play cat and mouse with me, Mister Long. My name is Judith Farnsworth. My kid brother, Rafe, came up from Denver with you aboard the same train, in his coffin. Do you need it any plainer than that?"

Longarm whistled softly, nodded soberly, and said, "Yep. I feel safe in giving you my word as an enlisted man and gentleman that I have never to my knowledge even met the late Raphael Farnsworth. So how in thunder could I have had one thing to do with his coming home in that box or any other condition?"

She sneered up at him and insisted, "Don't try to weasel out of it by arguing about who pulled the trigger. You were there, in command, when poor Rafe died like a dog without a chance to defend himself!"

He smiled thinly down at her and responded, "We'd best spell out who died like anything before we decide who might or might not be guilty of what, Miss Judith. I'll allow I'd like a peek inside that fancy coffin myself, before it's planted permanent in the sweet by-and-by. Were you planning on an open-casket ceremony, once you got whoever up by Trapper's Rock?"

She looked horrified and replied, "Heaven forfend! That could finish our poor father entire. He's suffered a bad fall and a brain-stroke since Rafe ran away, and I thought we'd just bury my brother more privately, here at the county seat, without telling the major about it."

He didn't answer.

She insisted, defensively, "It's not as if anyone would be fibbing to anyone. Since that brain-stroke the major's been sort of childish and forgetsome and, well, I'm not sure he remembers my brother turning out so bad. It might be just as well if he never does."

Longarm nodded but insisted, "I'd still like to know whether your kid brother's really dead or not. Where might you be hiding that box they shipped somebody in this afternoon?"

She stared up saucer-eyed and answered in an uncertain tone, "For land's sake, nobody's hiding it! Rafe and the coffin he's in are just down the street at Vandermeer's Funeral Chapel, and who else might you have killed down near Denver if it wasn't my poor wayward brother?"

He reached down to help her up to her own feet as he rose to his, saying, "Nobody named Rafe Farnsworth, to my knowledge. You can ask the undertakers to open the box or you can put me to the trouble of applying for a search warrant. Either way, I'm going to have me a gander inside that coffin."

She didn't answer. But as he moved toward the door, still holding her right hand with his left, she didn't resist. So he holstered his sixgun, saying, "*Bueno.* We'd both best leave our carbines here. Are you checked into this hotel or did you sneak up here, by the way?"

She looked indignant and protested, "It was you who checked in here after me. It was mighty dumb of you, after I'd already pegged some shots at you just down the street!"

He smiled sheepishly and said, "That'll teach me to check into the only decent hotel in town. You naturally saw me getting off the train when you went over to the depot to meet that coffin, right?"

She answered, primly, "I'd have killed you then and there, had I known who you were, as I saw you dropping down from the very car my poor dead brother came back to Boulder aboard. It was only after I got to talking to the train crew that I discovered the very man who'd killed him had followed after him to gloat and—"

"Aw, hang some crepe on your nose. Your brain just died," Longarm cut in, morosely. So she called him an unfeeling brute and went into a silent sulk as he led her downstairs and through the dimly lit little lobby.

Chapter 5

As they passed the desk that same clerk nodded sagely and called out, "Evening, Miss Judith. I see you caught up with Deputy Long in 214 like I said you might."

She didn't answer. Neither did Longarm. The clerk hadn't really told him anything he couldn't have figured on his own if it had been that important.

The true identity of the cadaver she seemed so intent on avenging was the most important question he had on his mind right now. Despite her sulk, or maybe because of the firm grip he had on her right arm now, Judith Farnsworth led the way to the funeral chapel at a good clip. Like most such establishments in an uncertain world, Vandermeer's was open twenty-four hours a day, if you didn't expect anything fancy after sundown. The owners and other big shots had naturally left for the day, but the front door was unlocked, and as Longarm herded the gal into a showroom filled with coffins plain and fancy, an elderly pale-faced gent who looked as if he'd just climbed out of one came from the back, buttoning his frock coat as he smiled at them uncertainly.

Longarm said, "Howdy. To save misunderstood discussions, I am the law, federal, and this here's Miss Judith Farnsworth, a customer of this establishment."

The mortuary attendant nodded understandingly and said, "If either of you would like to pay respects to the Farnsworth boy, we have him in our mauve chamber. I'll be only too happy to lead the way."

He didn't really look so happy as they followed him through an archway and along a dark corridor that smelled as if they'd tried to do something with pine oil but hadn't used enough. The musty old man with the sickly sweet breath of Mister Death clinging to his frock coat, or maybe shoes, led them into a small stuffy side chamber lit by jasmine-scented candles and, sure enough, papered with a deep-purple floral design on a lighter mauve background. The mahogany coffin on a couple of sawhorses against the far wall was the same one his saddle had come up from Denver aboard. He turned to the old-timer and said, simply, "We'd like you to open the lid for us now."

He was braced for an argument. But unlike Mike, the baggage-smasher aboard the train, this old bird was apparently used to such morbid curiosity, and better yet, knew how to get a coffin open without a set of burglar tools.

As Longarm watched the attendant twist a discreet screw here and there, he felt obliged to say, "I admire a man who knows his job, no matter what his job may be. Do all these boxes open the same way?"

Pleased at the compliment, the older man smiled shyly and confided, "Not hardly. Each maker has his own ideas on the subject. But since it was our usual associates down in Denver who, ah, prepared this client for shipment—"

"At whose direction?" Longarm asked, turning back to the girl with a quizzical eyebrow raised as the old-timer—who was only watching the corpses at night, after all—replied that they'd know more about that in the office come morning.

Judith explained, "I was the one who ordered Rafe

58

shipped home in this model coffin. I chose it from amid the samples out front when I came in to make the arrangements."

Longarm asked when, and how come.

She snapped, "This morning at the crack of dawn, because Rafe was dead, of course. I got the wire from Denver at our home spread about this time last night. Thank God it was me and not our gabby ramrod who signed for the delivery. I rode down from the Rocking F with the young gent from Western Union and . . ."

Then the attendant swung the the coffin lid open and she gasped, "Hold on, that's not my brother, Rafe! I've never seen this dead gentleman in my life before!"

Longarm had, though the corpse-washers down in Denver had treated the owlhoot rider to a spanking new suit, shirt, and tie as well as a shave, haircut, and more face powder than a decent woman ever wore to church. When Judith repeated that they'd sold her a perfect stranger in a mighty expensive package, Longarm told her, "He was neither perfect nor a stranger, at least to me, Miss Judith. Allow me to present the late Rafe Wade. Lord knows where they shipped his dead brother, Lem. I suspicion both were killed by Bart Larkin, so's he could lay the blame for some other crimes on a couple of kids who couldn't argue back."

She demanded, "Then where's my kid brother?"

Longarm told her, "It beats me. Like I told you before, I never heard of your fool brother until this evening. I hope you see, now, how unlikely it is that I've done one damned thing to you and your own that I deserve to die for!"

She started to say something dumb. But since she wasn't really dumb she blanched and said, "Oh, my God! If I'd really managed to kill you, back at the hotel just now, Mister Long . . ."

He said, "My mamma named me Custis. Don't ask me why. I've a much better notion why somebody wired a worried older sister that I was on my way up here with her baby brother, after killing him, now that I've seen how, ah, impulsive you can get with a gun in your hands."

She demanded to know who could have played such a dirty joke on her.

He said, "I just now implied the joke was meant to be on *me*. But you're right about it being dirty. Do you have that wire you got from Denver about the demise of your brother, Rafe?"

She said it was back at the hotel. Then she turned to the old gray gent who worked there and said, "We're going to have to work something out about the deposit I made here, sir. You see, this body they sent us seems to be the wrong one and . . . "

"That's why they ask for a deposit up front, ma'am," said the old attendant with the weary smile of someone who'd had similar conversations in the past. He added, "I've been listening. I'm sure Mister Vandermeer will feel as sorry about all this as I do. On the other hand, we and our Denver associates acted in good faith, and it's not as if we can just say oops and put everything back the way it was."

The confused and somewhat spoiled young cattle woman stuck out her lower lip and set her well-formed jaw more stubbornly. But before she could cloud up and rain all over anybody, Longarm took her by that arm again and said, "I want you to show me that wire from Denver now. This gent only works here, and it'll be up to the owners to settle for your deposit or sue you."

She said they'd better not as the old attendant shot him a grateful look. She let Longarm lead her, or at least gently drag her, back outside. Once they were alone and he'd explained how seldom any undertaker sued anyone, after mixing up one cadaver with another, she seemed more willing to quit while she was ahead. She fell in step beside him, and while he was braced for some dumb remarks about entering a hotel lobby late at night with a man who'd never been introduced properly to her kin, she never made them. It wouldn't have been polite to ask her how often she behaved so freely in and about the county seat. So he never did. That desk clerk had wandered off somewhere again. So they just went on up the stairs to her room, that being where she had the wire saying her kid brother lay dead in the Denver Morgue if she wanted to do anything about it.

Her room, down the hall from his, was furnished much the same. He saw she'd draped her saddlebags over the foot of her own brass bed.

She got out the wire, and a bottle of Jack Daniels while she was at it. The hotel supplied two tumblers and a pitcher of branch water from her corner washstand. He planted his hat and his rump on her bed covers as he scanned the mysterious telegram while she poured. He said to go easy on that infernal water, since he'd eaten a hearty supper and her whiskey was a known brand.

The wire, long enough to have cost the joker dearly at day rates, simply said Raphael Farnsworth, Junior, of Trapper's Rock lay dead and unclaimed in Denver after losing an argument with a posse of Indian Nation and Colorado lawmen led by the notorious Longarm. It offered to have a respectable Denver undertaker embalm, box, and run the body up to Vandermeer's in Boulder, subject to approval by the next of kin. It was signed, "Rafe's friend, Jake," but directed Judith and no other next of kin to contact Vandermeer, there in Boulder, and let them work things out. As Judith handed him his heroic drink he said, "Pretty slick. I'll have my own pals in Denver ask the usual questions at the morgue and that other undertaker's, but I'll be mighty surprised if our prankster went anywhere near either. Knowing a dead boy called Rafe was on ice in the morgue, knowing you had a runaway kid brother named Rafe, as well as a hasty temper—"

"It sounds awfully risky," she cut in, sitting down at his side atop the covers to clink tumblers with him. "Look how many things could have gone wrong. The morgue down in Denver might have insisted both the last name and first name had to match up. The real Rafe, I mean *our* Rafe, could have just written home, or for that matter *come* home. So then where would the mean joker have been?"

Longarm sipped thoughtfully and replied, "Just as safe, whether his cruel stunt worked or not. My ears still ring every time I recall how close it came to working."

He didn't add that he suspected he knew how the rascal who'd sent that false message might have guessed the real Raphael Farnsworth wouldn't be back at the Rocking F to spoil the fun. That baggage-smasher had been right about the average number of Rafes one met up with on your average day. A lot of outlaws took the *noms de guerre* of more innocent gents who'd wound up dead. He asked Judith to tell him more about her wild kid brother without explaining just why.

It took them another round of drinks before he had the all-too-sad old story down pat. Like his older sister, who was maybe twenty-three or twenty-four, Rafe Farnsworth had grown up comfortable if not downright sheltered on their father's big mountain spread up between Ward and Jamestown. Longarm knew the area and some of their neighbors, thanks to having worked up near Trapper's Rock on a post office robbery one time. So he knew it was a swell part of the country to raise kids. Judith allowed they'd both had their own remudas of cow ponies, and that even though the major had expected them to pitch in with the chores and ride drag at roundup times, the hired help had seen to it that neither of the boss man's kids ever suffered injury or even serious sweat. She said, and Longarm tended to agree, it might have been the softer than average work with his daddy's cows that young Rafe had found too tedious to abide. Rafe hadn't needed pocket jingle, she said, as much as he'd apparently pined for pure excitement. At any rate, he'd run off, without leaving any farewell messages, although, she now remembered, a rider off a neighboring spread had run into Rafe up near Lyons and repeated the boy's odd notions about going to college up that way.

Longarm asked her to try and repeat that stuff about a college near Lyons in more detail. "I know there's no college up in that part of the county, if we're talking about real ones. But that might not have been exactly what he meant."

She said, "I figured that out a long time ago. Old Lefty might have gotten things mixed up and thought Rafe meant a school near Lyons when he was really talking about somewhere else."

Longarm started to agree. Then he frowned thoughtfully down into his drink and asked if they could be talking about Lefty of the Middle Fork, a bronc peeler about his own age and with common sense. When she said that sure did sound like the same Lefty, Longarm told her, "I know him of old from another trackdown. Lefty of the Middle Fork gave me some mighty good leads after he'd fixed me up with some mighty fine horseflesh. If Lefty says your brother told him about some sort of college up near Lyons, then your kid brother told him about some kind of college up near Lyons."

She said, "But Custis, there isn't any college or even a trade school up near Lyons. It's mostly a market town, serving the surrounding mining or cattle operations. I doubt there's more than a thousand souls in or about Lyons on a Saturday night!"

He said, "It's a tad bigger town than that. But you're right about local opportunities for higher education. If I could have just a few more drops of that Jack Daniels, I'd be proud to tell you about the rogue your kid brother might have met up with. I already noticed that wire must have been sent to you by some half-wit who considers his fool self smarter than the rest of us."

She refreshed her own glass while she was at it, neglecting to add water to either this time. He didn't care. Good whiskey didn't need much cutting, once you got over the first jolt. She listened intently as he brought her up to date on Professor Jethro Markham. Once he had, she repressed a shudder and said, "Oh, Lord, now I'm really worried about poor Rafe! I don't see why you call such a master criminal a half-wit, though. Seems to me a man capable of half the things he's pulled off has to be as good as his brag!"

Longarm looked disgusted and replied, "They're never as good as they brag, and a master criminal is a contradiction in common sense."

He was sorry he'd said that as soon as she asked why. He told her she didn't really need a lecture on the wages of sin, seeing it was her kid brother and not her who'd run off to lead a life of crime. It seemed needlessly harsh to add he suspected the poor little shit could be dead if the professor was assigning his name to other pupils. He said, "Well, it's getting late and whatever your own plans were, after killing me, I got a heap of paperwork and a considerable cross-country ride ahead of me come morning. So I'll just fetch your gun from under my bed, down the hall, and—"

"You can't leave me alone and undefended!" she protested. "Not now that you've told me what awful company Rafe could be keeping company with!"

Longarm didn't spell out all his reasons when he assured her he doubted her kid brother was unlikely to be after either of them. He pointed out, "You're the only one here in Boulder who's pegged any shots at me, no offense."

She rose with him as he got to his feet. She clutched at his sleeves, belly to belly with him, as she insisted, wide-eyed, "That evil Jethro Markham must know where both of us are this very minute. How else could he have planned to trick me into killing you?"

Longarm said, "He only needed your home address and the fact that I'd be likely headed up this way. We just proved how many things could go wrong with such half-baked mischief, Miss Judith."

But she insisted, "By now he knows his first grand notion didn't work. If he has the brains of a gnat he's also figured out that once we put our heads together, friendly, we'd both wind up knowing more than either of us could have known before."

Longarm smiled down at her and said, "I'd really like to put our heads together, closer. But I doubt I'd catch up with the sly old rascal that way."

She asked him how he'd ever be sure if he never tried it, and stood on tiptoe to throw both arms around his neck and haul his head down for a good wet smack. He gave her some tongue as well, seeing that was the way she wanted to kiss, and it seemed only natural to plant a big palm on either of her firm buttocks as she ground the fly of her men's jeans against his tweed pants. He could tell as he did so that she had nothing on under the thin sun-faded denim. But as they came up for air, at last, he felt obliged to point out, "This hasn't a thing to do with that college for crime up near Lyons, or even those carbines in my own room."

She pleaded in both words and motions for another kiss. He held her tighter but told her, "Come rain or come shine, I'm heading out on horseback tomorrow, you impulsive as well as pretty little thing."

She nodded, thrust her pubic bone against him, harder, and purred, "I never said I meant to take you home to meet my kith and kin, Custis. I just need someone big and strong to get me through this scary night in town!"

He was getting hard himself, and this time, when they kissed, they somehow seemed to wind up sprawled across the bed. She hadn't exactly said whether she was scared somebody else might bust in on her if he left her alone, or whether she'd bust if she had to spend a night alone in this swell bed. Longarm had noticed, in many another hotel, how sliding bare between cool clean sheets atop a firm mattress aboard springs that didn't squeak could inspire a raging erection way before you could count a hundred fool sheep.

From the way the slim suntanned brunette was wriggling out of her riding outfit without rolling out of his friendly arms he suspected, with an irrational jealous pang, that she wasn't used to sleeping alone if it could possibly be avoided. He was able to undress his own fool self in this position as well, although getting shed of the gun rig and boots without letting go of her was a bitch, and then they had both pillows under her horsewoman's hips and he was posting in her love saddle with her clinging to the horn. The rules of riding a bucking bronco and a bucking beauty were indeed reversed.

He tried to hold back a mite, out of consideration for the feelings of a lady. But she kept begging him to do it faster, spurring him to do so with her nails digging into his already inspired rump. So in point of fact he came in her almost at once, but saw at once that he'd been needlessly concerned. For she came, on his quivering afterglow, and then they were off and jumping fences together after the elusive and all-too-fleeting pleasures of strangers in the night.

He didn't want her to, but later, as they were sharing a smoke side by side, with the covers pulled over their glowing flesh at last, Judith felt obliged, as most women seemed to, to explain how they'd just wound up in bed together. Most women considered it a point of honor never to admit they'd just felt like some screwing and thought you might be the sort of gent who could satisfy a lady in need of the same. That might have made the cuss they were in bed with at the moment feel pleased with himself as well as the way things had turned out.

. Since their rules forbade such coddling of the other side, gals who'd just come moaning and groaning with a gent liked to tell him they were only in this ridiculous position because some other cruel cuss had been mistreating them and they wanted revenge, or as in this one's case, because she'd meant to be a nun or at least a schoolmarm until some long-donging skunk had broken her in and then lit out on her just as she was getting to like it and never wanted to stop.

As Longarm blew a weary smoke ring at the fancy pressed-tin ceiling somewhere up there in the darkness, Judith confided, "I have to be mighty discreet about this sort of thing, living in the country where the nosey neighbors gossip about the love life of their livestock. But there's an older and more discreet rider, here and about betwixt Ward and Jamestown, that a maiden in distress can trust."

He didn't want to know whether Lefty of the Middle Fork had been over this range ahead of him. He asked what in thunder there was to gossip about when livestock got down to it.

She wriggled closer and began to fondle him some more as she explained, "They only pass along unusual love affairs of critters. For example there's this Dutch shopkeeper up in Ward who raises eating rabbits in hutches out back. You know how anxious rabbits are to screw and so anyway, this old maid just up the street has a big fat tabby cat, and when she gets in heat, the only tomcat in the neighborhood having been shot for practice by one of the Roberts twins—"

"I've heard jackrabbits will trifle with a willing cat," he cut in. "That's not how you get them funny-looking Manx cats, though, no matter who tells you."

She said those same Roberts twins had tried to get a billy goat to rut with a mastiff bitch in heat, only the big canine had ripped its would-be lover's throat out the moment he'd tried to mount her.

He said, "Those Roberts twins sound like a bundle of laughs. Might they have been pals of your kid brother's, before he ran off?"

She sighed and said, "Not hardly. For all his faults, my brother, Rafe, was a couple of years older and at least one brain smarter than both the Roberts twins combined. You might call the two of them, together, the village idiot of Ward. My brother, Rafe, was just bored and restless, not retarded."

He said, "*Bueno*. I wasn't looking forward to riding that far out of my way. Since those Roberts twins confine their crimes to cruelty to animals, I'll only ride you partway home if you'd like to hang around town until I compare a few notes with the sheriff's department."

She began to stroke him thoughtfully as she replied that

she'd love him to ride her at least as far as this one aspen glade she knew of, up the Trapper's Rock trail a ways. Then she added, "I'm not sure I want any sheriff's deputies knowing about us riding off through the trees together, though. Like I said, a girl in my position has to be discreet."

He told her he'd have her in a mighty discreet position if she kept fooling with his old organ-grinder like that. Then when she didn't, he decided, "I reckon I could excuse us riding off together to both the local sheriff and my boss down in Denver if you had a recent photograph of your missing brother. No offense, but I got to put him on our list of possible suspects, witnesses, or whatever."

She said, "As a matter of fact Rafe and Lucky Lem Corrigan of the Diamond E had their pictures taken together, here in town, just before Rafe left home without a word of explanation. I'd hate to part with our only copy, though."

He patted her bare shoulder and soothed, "You won't have to, seeing as a photographer here in Boulder would have the negative on file unless he's a total fool. Who might this Lucky Lem be, the late Rafe Wade having a brother called Lem Wade, and ain't *that* curious as hell."

She sighed and said, "Oh, Lucky Lem was a friend, a mighty good friend, to both my brother and me. He never mentioned having any brothers or even sisters, though."

Longarm took a thoughtful pull on his cheroot and didn't ask how come they called Lem Corrigan "Lucky." He figured he'd guessed right when she gave his semi-erection another playful pull and added, "Lucky said he'd write, but he never did, after he took that better job up along the South Saint Vrain."

Her grip on another man's virility got almost painful as she added, bitterly, "I reckon Trapper's Rock seemed too far to mess with, once the good-looking rascal got into Lyons of a Saturday night, huh?"

Longarm told her, quietly, "Sometimes life turns out more complicated than we think. Neither Rafe nor Lem are usual names, like Tom, Dick, or Harry. If one young outlaw inspired by an older crook was using your kid brother's first name as an alias, who's to say the one calling himself Lem Wade didn't steal the first part from your, ah, old friend Lucky Lem Corrigan?"

She propped herself up on one elbow to stare down at him wild-eyed, demanding, "Are you saying my Lem, the real Lem, might have meant to write, might have meant all he said to me before he left for that other job, only he never did because he couldn't, because . . . Oh, Custis, whatever could have happened to my poor darling Lucky Lem?"

"Mayhaps his luck ran out," Longarm suggested. "Did your kid brother turn up missing before or after your, this, ah, other rider lit out for other parts?"

She thought, then said, "Lucky told us about this job as a head wrangler, up the other side of Lyons, and then one day he just wasn't around Trapper's Rock any more. It was while he was asking about Lucky, up in Lyons, that Rafe heard tell of this professor who taught young gents about more adventurous ways to get ahead in the world. I never thought Rafe meant to sign up. When he told me about it he laughed and said it sounded sort of wild. But after he lit out like that I asked around, and discovered he'd bragged some to younger riders about the wild pals he might or might not have up along the South Saint Vrain."

Longarm noticed his cheroot was about finished and that she'd let go of his old ring-dang-doo in talking about other sons of bitches she'd likely jerked hard in her time. So he told her, "It's too early to say what might or might not have happened to either old boy of which you speak, honey lamb. Like I said, the photographer who took that picture of the two of 'em together ought to have the glass negative. So I'll get him to run me off a copy, and once I'm up around Lyons I'll have something to show folks as well as something to look for. Meanwhile, it's getting late and what say we finish off right and get some shut-eye."

But as he put her bare hand back on his naked privates she snatched it away as if he'd offered her a red-hot poker and demanded, "Are you mad, you unfeeling brute? First you tell me I could have been wrong, wrong, wrong about my darling Lucky Lem, and then you try to get fresh with me. What kind of a girl do you think I am?"

He muttered, "Impulsive," since it would have been the mark of a sore loser, accurate or not, to call her a woman scorned as well. As he sat up on his side of the bed and swung his bare feet to the rug she seemed to think it mattered as she weakly giggled and said, "I suppose that sounded sort of silly, coming from me, after all I've just let you do to my weak flesh."

He rose to stride over to the washstand, not looking back as he replied, "I'm sure sorry I had to use all that brute force on you, ma'am. Shall we save the explanations or, God forbid, confessions? I follow your drift. A handsome cowhand who hung out with your brother broke you in to the forbidden fun of fornication, no doubt with the heap of love words and promises it takes the first few times, and then, when you thought he'd betrayed you, you set out to betray him back with all the discreet doings you felt you might get away with. It's an old familiar story, and I agree most men deserve to be sent to bed without no supper for the way they make little girls cry."

She insisted, "Damn it, Custis, until just now I really did think he'd made a perfect fool of me. I never considered that something bad might have happened to him!"

Longarm started to point out that the odds were still way the hell against her. Ninety-nine times out of a hundred a gent who ran off and left a lady in the lurch was the louse she thought he was. But Longarm was no fool. So he quit while he was ahead, and got to falling asleep in the end with a locked door between him and this impulsive little thing.

Chapter 6

Longarm woke up around sunrise because a pair of teamsters were having it out with bullwhips down in the street and, once he'd noticed that, because he had to enjoy a good leak and some breakfast, in that order. It seemed there was nothing like high-altitude screwing to inspire a ravenous appetite—in the one who'd done most of the work at any rate. Longarm didn't rap on Judith's door on his way downstairs, once he'd gotten half shaved and fully dressed. If they could fix him up with say a sepia-tone of her missing brother and lover, there was nothing else she could do for him—in the way of evidence at any rate. He suspected that should he offer to ride her all the way home, the distance being a good ten miles or more, he could likely get her to show him that aspen grove she'd mentioned. But on the other hand, aspen groves tended to be infested with ticks, she'd likely laid more than one other cuss in such a discreet place, and he was never going to get to Lyons if he went sniffing after females in another direction, damn it.

He ordered fried eggs over *jigote* with an order of cheese-cake to wash down with his third cup of black coffee. The fat waitress from the night before had been replaced by a pretty little thing Longarm might have taken for her daughter, had she been half as nice. He tipped her a nickel anyway, to show that her sullen ways and the way she'd fried his eggs too crisp on the edges and too runny in the centers hadn't really pissed him.

Few of the shops in the center of Boulder were open yet. Both the local and county lockups were, since they never closed. The night crew still on duty at the sheriff's department found his visit a welcome novelty. He had no trouble establishing that while the badges flashed in the Denver Parthenon by the so-called deputies Wade and Steele had likely been genuine or at least honorary, the printed-up I.D. cards they'd both had on them had looked nothing at all like the ones his new pals and fellow peace officers had been issued by Boulder County. As he scanned the I.D. a helpful file clerk held out for his inspection, Longarm mused aloud, although half to himself, "This explains the sudden panic in the Parthenon of our so-called Deputy Steele. But had he shown the fool card he had to that newspaper man, he'd have likely gotten away with it. I took their I.D. at face value until just now. They even had the county seal, in pastel, under the heavier ink of fancy type set by some professional printer, I'm sure."

After he'd gone on to point out a dozen ways those I.D.'s failed to match this real one, the deputy in charge of the front-office files said, "I'm pretty sure our own I.D. cards were set in type and run off by some printer." He half turned to call out to the desk man in the next room toward the front entrance. That deputy couldn't say who did the printing for the sheriff's department either, but suggested they'd surely know at the hall of records across the way.

Longarm smiled thinly and said, "I'm sure they would. Meanwhile, I doubt anyone setting type for Boulder County would tell me they were whipping up fake I.D. for crooks, and if they *were* doing anything that wild, I imagine they'd do a better job, don't you?"

The local lawman started to ask a dumb question. Then he brightened and said, "Hey, you're right. One of our regular printers, turned bad on us, would have only had to run off a few extra cards and save 'em, blank. Even if he had to start from scratch, saying the crooks who needed fake I.D. showed up after the job was done with and out of the printing plant . . . "

"Exactly." Longarm nodded. "At the very least they'd have used the same typeface, card stock, and such. So let's go with a jackass describing a deputy's I.D. he's seen somewhere, from memory."

"What if he described a good one, only not one issued by this here county?" asked the man from the Boulder sheriff's department.

Longarm stared soberly at the younger and greener-looking lawman to flatly opine, "I see a grand future for you in this game, old son. I was dumb as hell not to wait around for photographs of those fake deputies and their I.D.'s. You see what they mean about haste making waste. Until this very minute it never occurred to me that they might have whipped up fake I.D. cards by copying real ones from some other county. If I had some pictures to flash around . . . But I don't, and like they say about that too, if the dog hadn't stopped to shit it might have caught the rabbit."

The Boulder County deputies agreed.

Longarm glanced at their Regulator Brand wall clock and added, "I'd better quit shitting and get it on up the trail. I suspect all this razzle-dazzle with made-up names and false I.D. is designed to slow me down. I confess I hesitated to compare notes with you boys when it occurred to me at least a couple of real Boulder County lawmen could be riding for the other side."

They agreed it seemed a pure bitch and that there ought to be a law against slickers like Professor Jethro Markham, wherever the hell he was hiding out in Boulder County, if that was where he was.

Longarm asked about photograph galleries and when they

suggested one just around the corner, that was where he headed next. But once he got there they'd never heard of young Rafe Farnsworth or his handsome pal, Lucky Lem.

He did better at The Photostudio of Doctor Daguerre, across from the municipal corral. It was closer to Western Union and, better yet, the proprietor recalled taking that picture of the two missing riders without having to look it up in his files. He said, in plain English with mayhaps a New England twang, that he set aside portraits of cowboys and Indians for posterity. Longarm felt no call to ask what posterity was apt to want with pictures of cowboys and Indians. He showed his badge and I.D. and explained some of his reasons for wanting at least one paper print of his own.

The Yankee sporting the distinguished French name told him he could whip up half a dozen within the hour for five dollars. He said he hardly figured it was worth getting out all the chemicals and such for less, but that once he was set up in back, Longarm could have all the sepia-tones he wanted for two bits extra, each.

The tall deputy dryly observed half a dozen prints ought to do him, and that he'd be back for them once he'd seen if there were any night letters for him at the nearby Western Union.

There weren't. As long as he was there, Longarm sent Billy Vail an update, asked some questions, and allowed it seemed safe to contact him next in care of the telegraph office in Lyons, now that it didn't look like the sheriff of Boulder County was in cahoots with Professor Jethro Markham, after all.

He still didn't see how the lifer could have walked out of that Iowa prison as another prisoner entire unless more than one prison official had been corrupted, blind drunk, or both. He was still waiting on both photographs and complete physical descriptions of the crooks they'd mixed up so astoundingly, but unless they'd been identical twins, which hardly seemed likely, there was simply no excuse that Longarm, for one, would accept. He well recalled the hell Billy Vail had raised the time that escape artist had razzle-dazzled his way out of the federal house of detention in Denver, when somebody on duty that confusing morning had simply opened the front door for him.

Hoping his home office might beat him up to Lyons by wire with something he could use, Longarm strode back to the photographer's to see how those photographs were coming. The owner had all six of them drying out on blotting paper when Longarm got back. That figured to be way more than he'd ever need, and when the photographer told him fancy pasteboard frames that you could stand up like easels only cost a dime extra each, Longarm told him not to push his luck and paid off with a golden half eagle, saying, "That's five silver cartwheels I'd like back, and let's see what I just bought at such an outrageous price."

The photographer gingerly picked up one sepia-tone print and placed it on the counter in front of Longarm, saying, "They really ought to dry at least an hour before anyone handles 'em. We've come a long way since my father invented photography, but it's still best not to rush things."

Longarm left the damp print in place as he stared soberly down at it. He didn't want to get into just how Louis-Jacques-Mandé Daguerre might have fathered New England Yankees in France, where he'd been born close to a hundred years ago. It was hard to say whether the younger of the two riders grinning up at him in sepia-tone bore a family resemblance to Judith Farnsworth. Just about everyone with regular features and dark hair and eyes looked related. It was easier to see which one had to be Lucky Lem Corrigan. He was closer to Longarm's age and build and not a bad-looking cuss, if one could abide a man who shaved his upper lip and fixed his light brown hair in a sort of spit curl under his ten-gallon hat, as if he thought he was Napoleon, for Pete's sake. The bigger giveaway was the pair of fancy batwing chaps he'd put on to show everyone he was a real cowboy. There were three German silver conchos down each thigh, and they'd stitched a double L on the right flap and a brand Longarm read as Diamond E on the other. Lucky Lem was posing with two sixguns in a fancy buscadero rig of tooled cordovan leather too. Longarm muttered, "I'll bet he had the barber splash him with extra bay rum."

The self-styled son of Louis Daguerre said, "I wouldn't know. I don't allow any smoking back by the scenery. It's highly flammable, all the way from Chicago. To look at those two boys you'd never guess they were really here in this establishment and not out among those jagged peaks 'neath a threatening sky when I got 'em to hold still and watch the birdie a spell, right?"

Longarm allowed the backdrop the two pals were posed in front of looked at least as real as anything Currier and Ives had ever put on the market. He gingerly felt the paper stock in front of him. Daguerre said, "Don't! Not just yet. They'll dry in just a few more minutes at this altitude, but give 'em the time they need. It'd be a shame to mess up such fine craftsmanship by careless handling. Did I fail to mention I was the son of the man who invented the art?"

He must have read the amusement in Longarm's gun-muzzle gray eyes. He quickly added, "Born out of wedlock, I'll confess with no shame, since I'd rather be the bastard of a great man than the lawful son of, oh, say, some Yankee peddler who drank too much."

Longarm nodded soberly and replied, "I never said you were fibbing, Doctor Daguerre. It's easy to see old Louis Daguerre could have sired at least a few bastards around your age before he died back in, when, about the time of the California Gold Rush?"

"Close enough," said the eccentric son or mayhaps admirer of the daddy of them all. He began to go into a fable about his famous father's hitherto unrecorded visit to these shores. Longarm cut him short by conceding it stood to reason a high-born Yankee virgin should have lost her head with a slick-talking Frenchman who'd been older than fifty when he'd patented his famous invention in '39— or a good ten years after this poor cuss had been sired by that Yankee peddler he recalled so fondly, if Longarm was any judge of the wear and tear on the human face or the all-too-human tales they made up about themselves.

Longarm wasn't sure why so many folk, more than half, made up such whoppers about their fool selves. His job would have been tough enough if even half the folks he talked to told the truth, the whole truth, and nothing but the truth, the way they all said they did. To steer the conversation back to more important mysteries than the lineage of a small-town photographer, Longarm asked if "Daguerre Junior" could recall anything the two pals might have been jawing about the day they sat for their portrait. The older man shook his head and replied, "I get more business than that. I've photographed at least a dozen wedding parties and Lord knows how many christenings, and them constitutions they dress Roman Catholic kids up fancy for."

Longarm didn't see fit to explain confirmation rites to the love child of a famous Frenchman. The poor coot had already said his parents hadn't been married in any sort of church at all. Longarm said, "That's too bad. You see, both these old boys seem to have dropped out of sight, as far as their kith and kin here in Boulder can tell me. I was hoping they might have been planning to run off and be pirates when they grew up, whilst you were photographing 'em in their cowboy suits."

The photographer shrugged and replied, "Oh, Lucky Lem Corrigan is a real cowboy as well as a bit of a devil with the ladies, if you know what I mean. Young Rafe Farnsworth rides and ropes well enough, from what I hear. But between you and me, no son of no rich man is ever working at the family trade, even when he thinks he is."

Longarm smiled thinly and said, "It's lucky my folks was poor then. I turned out lazy enough as it is. I don't know what you mean about Lem Corrigan and the ladies. Tell me more about that."

The older man shot a guilty glance around the interior of his shop, as if afraid he'd get caught in the act of dishing the dirt, and said, "Well, you never heard it from me. But some do say Lucky Lem didn't really leave town because he landed a better job. They say he was messing with Miss Judith Farnsworth, and you know what they say about *her*!"

Longarm suspected he did, but he pasted an innocent smile on and replied, innocently, "I'm new here, and you just said Lucky Lem and young Rafe here were good pals."

"Daguerre Junior" smiled lewdly and observed, "If I had a nice new shiny dime for every young cuss who's ever messed with a pal's pretty sister, I'd be able to retire in style to my own private kingdom. But to tell the truth, or at least to tell it as I've heard it, Lucky Lem didn't have to worry about young Rafe finding out. It was *old* Rafe, the major, who'd have cleaned his plow for him if he'd known his daughter was messing with a mere hired hand off another spread."

Longarm nodded and said, "I heard Major Farnsworth has been feeling poorly of late."

The local man nodded soberly and said, "A lot of folk figure he's dying. My point is that until such time as you can count a rich man out entire, it's sort of dumb to screw his only daughter and then brag about it to your pals."

Longarm whistled softly, nodded, and said, "Two pals can keep a secret if one of them is dead. I can see how many here in town must have heard about the two lovebirds if *I* just did. Does Major Farnsworth have any known guns in particular riding for him, or don't the gossip cover such details?"

The older man pursed his lips and primly replied that he couldn't say, not being as given to gossip as some of the other shopkeepers up and down the street. Longarm didn't press it. Since Lucky Lem had already left town and he'd be leaving any minute, it hardly mattered just how strict little Judith's dear old dad might or might not be.

The sepia-tone prints were dry enough to put away now—in Longarm's opinion at any rate. So he tucked them in an inside pocket, shoved the change from his ten-dollar piece in his pants, and bade the illegitimate son of Louis Daguerre a sincere farewell. Then he left to hire himself the horseflesh he'd need to get it on up to Lyons.

The livery wasn't far. He'd dealt with them in the past, so it only took him the better part of half an hour to be on his way aboard a no-longer-young but solidly built paint gelding, with a younger but scrawnier cordovan mare called Brandy packing the modest supplies he'd just picked up from the general store next door. The spurhead town of Lyons lay only fifteen bumpy miles or so north of the county seat, if one traveled as the crow flies. The most direct trail covered more like twenty-odd miles, because of those bumps, while a rider figuring to circle some and drift down the South Saint Vrain into Lyons from the higher slopes to the west had a full day's ride cut out for his fool self, and this day was almost half shot. But that was what extra supplies were for and if push came to shove, he was set to camp out at least a week in the tangled timber up and down the South Saint Vrain.

Having worked for both Uncle Sam and Captain Good-night in these parts before, Longarm soon had his two ponies moving up a sort of sneaky trail to the northwest without having to ask directions. In the unlikely event anyone was laying for him along the more-traveled trail to Lyons from Boulder, they were in for a tedious wait indeed. As he wound the paint through the first aspens, hauling Brandy and his grub after him on a long lead, Indian file, he reflected on how this old game trail, seldom used by riders and never by anything as wide as a wagon, would take him fairly close to Trapper's Rock, or at least to Jamestown, from whence Trapper's Rock and mayhaps a couple of positions he'd never gotten around to with that passionate Judith would lay no more than a couple of hours' lope uphill—if she'd headed home by now and still wanted to lay him. He laughed at himself and confided to his mount, whose formal name escaped him, "You're sure lucky they cut your nuts off young, before you knew what they were there for, Paint. I swear there are times I wish I'd never found out why boys and girls were built so different. For I damn it just now heard how one man had to leave town, sudden, and there I go dwelling on the forbidden delights of a cranky old rich man's daughter!"

He was dying for a smoke too. But lighting up in aspen thick as this could cost you more than the pleasure was worth. The young aspen saplings brushing his stirrups to either side weren't too flammable, even later in the summer when they'd be drier. Green aspen wood was almost worthless in a stove and gave more smoke and stink in a camp fire than wet wool socks. But aspen never grew this thick unless it had reseeded an old burn-out, and sure enough, when you peered deep enough into the shimmering green gloom all around, you could spy a charred stump here and a whole damned log of well-seasoned charcoal there. A wildfire whipping through a stand of living trees tended to just singe them dead and pass on, leaving the green wood to dry out for a few years until it was really fit for firewood, or a really vicious forest fire. The green and silver leaves fluttering at him from either side wouldn't burn worth mention either, full of life as they were this early. But just off the trail in every direction a thick layer of yesteryear's fallen leaves lay tinder-dry and overdue for another good burn-out.

So Longarm studied on unanswered questions, tedious as they might be, instead of known pleasures that could get a man sidetracked, if not in real trouble. It wasn't easy. He was at that stage of the hunt where most hunters started talking about packing it in.

He settled for an unlit cheroot to chew on as he forged on, confiding to the patient paint pony, "I was a fidgety kid the first few times I went hunting, back home in West-by-God-Virginia, Paint. In case you've never hunted for the pot, it's only fun the first hour or so. By the time you've traipsed in vain through five or six miles of sticker bush, too hot if it's summer, too cold if it's winter, and never just right, you commence to suspect there just can't be any damned old deer or even a rabbit in these parts. That's when you quit if you're like most, and you're even more sure you've done right by the time you make it all the way back to camp, hungry, thirsty, footsore, and truly pissed at the assholes who ever told you there was anything worth hunting out this way in the first damn place."

He spied brighter light ahead and heeled the paint at a faster pace. As they burst out of the aspen into an open quarter section of ungrazed red clover and stirrup-deep blue columbines, with the snow-covered peaks of the Continental Divide grinning down at him from the cobalt western sky, he reined in to grin back and almost shout, "Good God almighty, ain't that pretty and ain't this a swell time and place to be alive and feeling tolerable?"

Neither pony answered, of course, but as they both lowered their muzzles to inhale lush greenery, Longarm reached for a match and let 'em, at least until he'd lit up and inhaled some himself. Then he dismounted and changed saddles while he had everyone in such a good mood. He let them graze a few minutes more, then swung himself back into his McClellan, aboard the cordovan mare this time, as he told them both, "We've got to get it on up the trail now. You can have some more grass this side of, let's say, two-thirty or three. But we'd best go easy on that clover this early in the season."

Brandy didn't want to stop stuffing herself with sweet clover blossoms and succulent stems. She tried to bite his right foot off when he cranked her head up with a firm but fair grip on the reins. He kicked her in the teeth instead. She decided the toes of his stove-pipe boots just weren't meant for a herbivorous critter after all, and agreed to go on, once he had her barrel head all the way up out of the infernal flowers.

He made a mental note that the paint would be best to have under him at tenser times along this trail. Meanwhile, they had most of the trail still ahead of him, and it was just too swell a day to feel pissed about anything as natural as a lively plug with a tough mouth and stubborn streak. The columbine-spangled greenup had wiped out the trail across the open glade, but Longarm knew about where they'd pick it up among the lodgepoles along the crest of that rise to the north, so that was the way he rode, tugging the lead line harder when he noticed the paint behind him plowing its fool muzzle through all that too tempting clover. He called back, "Cut that out, you nutless wonder. I let you both enjoy all the horse ice cream you ought to have for now. I swear, I don't see how you critters ever got along in this cruel world before my kind domesticated you. How many times does a horse have to suffer a bellyache before it sinks in that that uncured clover affects your guts about the same as green apples affect *our* guts, only worse, because we can burp way better than you."

They topped the rise, and the problem solved itself as they wound through tall timber over tasteless pine duff and bitter scrub cedar for a spell. Then they were crossing yet another sunny open stretch again, only now there were cows grazing all around and neither of his ponies seemed too tempted by the resultant stubble. Longarm read their brands as Lazy H Bar Z, and noted the herd was way oversized for the amount of grass that this particular mountain park provided. But while the Bureau of Land Management was federal, the abuse of open range wasn't a crime he was usually called upon to deal with. The gut and git grazing of the Lazy H Bar Z would have caused a heap more damage down on the High Plains to the east, where the shortgrass grew way slower on way less rain. So what the hell.

As he walked his mare up the far slope at a gentle walk, the slope getting steeper as they climbed, he heard the distant tinny tinkle of a Judas bell, and sure enough, a few minutes later, the yapping of a sheepdog. Cows never wore bells that tinklesome, and dogs barked different when they were talking to somebody other than sheep. He gazed all about to regather his bearings, and recalled there was indeed a narrow trail running along the wooded ridge he was fixing to cross over, bound for the cattle country beyond.

By recent agreement, after some nasty incidents between Colorado cattlemen and more recent stockmen who preferred to raise sheep, the public grazing up there in the Front Range had been divided fairly, as far as the state legislature saw it, by allowing cows to graze below the timberline, as they always had, with the sheep herds confined to the cooler but grassy enough slopes above the timberline.

Nothing could graze above the timberline between, say, early October and late April, of course. So Colorado sheep spent the cooler months down on the High Plains, at their owners' expense. It was the free grass up yonder to his left that Longarm figured the unseen sheepherder ahead had to be headed for. He reined in, just downslope from the tree line, to let the sheepherder or at least that dog take some notice of him and the ponies before they met up. Sheep, sheepdogs, and sheepherders all tended to spook when meeting up with riders in tall timber unexpectedly. Sheep and sheepdogs seemed to think ponies were some sort of sheep-eating beasts. Sheepherders had more reason to feel proddy in the company of men dressed more cow than *they* were. Some of those nasty incidents had been nasty as hell.

As if to prove Longarm's point, a handgun sounded off amid the trees up yonder and he heard someone whistle sharply to that dog and call out, hoarsely, "No! Don't kill my poor Scotty, mister! I swears to God he don't bite!"

Longarm muttered, "Aw, shit," and heeled on up the slope, calling out as he drew his own sixgun and fired at the sky for attention, "Here comes a paid-up peace officer, boys. So let's all keep the peace around here if we know what's good for us!"

As he crested the rise, gun still in hand, he wasn't at all surprised by the familiar and all too tedious tableau spread out amid the gray-green aspen boles all about him.

To his right stood a weary-looking old sheepherder, hold-

83

ing the lead of the jackass he had hitched to a two-wheeled cart. Down the slope behind him a border collie that had to be called Scotty was trying to keep about a hundred head of merinos bunched as it kept one eye on its master at the same time.

To Longarm's left the trio of cowhands he'd sort of expected sat their nervous ponies, as Longarm called out, not unkindly, "Howdy, boys. I'd be Deputy U.S. Marshal Custis Long, and now I'd like you all to put them guns away."

One rider, wearing a red velveteen shirt and an expression just as stupid, called back, "How do we know you're the law and not a sheep-lover, stranger?"

Longarm snorted in disgust and called back, "I just now told you who I was. Now, in case you haven't grasped it yet, I'd best tell you I still have four in the wheel of this .44–40 I'm pointing your way and I mean to drop you with the first round if you don't put that cap pistol of your own away this goddamn instant."

So after the three of them had holstered their side arms Longarm nodded approvingly and did the same so he could haul out his billfold and flash his badge at everyone. "Now that I see we're all going to be civilized about this, who'd like to tell me just what this is all about?"

One of the cowhands, this one dressed more sensibly, pointed at the old man down by the cart and said, "That sheep-screwing son of a bitch is trespassing on our range, as anyone can plainly see!"

The sheepherder started to cuss right back. But Longarm raised his free hand to demand, "Order in the court. To begin with, unless I'm lost entire, which I ain't, this ridge and the trails running over or along it are all on open rangeland, owned and managed to the extent anyone's supposed to manage it by the U.S. Department of the Interior."

The red-shirted rider off the Lazy H Bar Z protested, "Open range or not, it's us and nobody else around here who's using it right now, Uncle Sam."

Longarm smiled at him and his pals in a fatherly way and replied, "That oversight could be corrected, if I was to write to the same office where I sure hope you sent your grazing fees in full. But we was talking about sheep on a public right of way, not how many head of beef you're supposed to have out here on all this government grass, right?"

The three young cowhands exchanged worried looks. The sensibly dressed one asked, "What was that about a public whatever, Marshal?"

To which Longarm replied with a modest smile, "I'm only a deputy marshal. It's my boss, Marshal Billy Vail, you'll be in trouble with if he ever finds out you've tried to block an established trail across federal land."

Pointing at the lone sheep man to his right, he added, "Anyone can see this gent and his pup have a herd of their own to take up to the high country. This trail leads up to the bare slopes around Sawtooth Peak, unless I'm lost as hell. That's above the timberline. Meaning it's sheep country that sheepmen and cattlemen have both voted on, and what could be fairer than that?"

The one in the red shirt protested, "That well may be, but we just now caught them fool sheep grazing grass down here, along the way."

The sheepherder wailed that there was just no way one man and his dog could keep that many sheep from picking even one damned wildflower below the timberline. Longarm shushed him. "I know. I'm sure these other gents know too, unless those are bears or some other sort of meat-eater they're riding."

The three young hands had to chuckle at that picture. Longarm said, "I just now had a hell of a time getting these two ponies through uncured clover without letting 'em have enough to bloat on, I hope. If I was grazing beef around here, and didn't want to share a blade more grass with sheep than I had to, I reckon I'd be anxious to see those sheep safely on their way. I don't see why in thunder I'd want to stop 'em or, God forbid, *scatter* 'em! So why don't you boys just ride on, and I feel sure this other gent will be off any range you could possibly be grazing by sundown."

Two of them shifted in their saddles as if considering his notion at least. The one in the red shirt sat still, his lower lip stuck out like a stubborn brat's. So Longarm said, "Let me put it this way. I'm fixing to start counting, silent, to myself. So there's just no way of saying just how far I mean to count before I draw again and this time shoot to kill, is there?"

Then he stuck a fresh cheroot in his bared teeth and just stared at them until, sure enough, one muttered, "Come on, pards, he just might mean it." The three of them spun their mounts around to light out to the northwest, down the far slope.

Longarm turned back to the old sheepherder and said, "There you go. I don't want to ride up to Sawtooth Peak with nobody. I can keep you company as far as the cross trail to Jamestown though, if you're worried about those boys."

The sheepherder shook his head and said, "I ain't worried. You may not know how unsettling you stare at gents, but I'm sure they noticed and I'm sure we've seen the last of that bunch. Who are them two riders over to the southeast though?"

Longarm turned in his saddle to glance back the way he'd just come, without seeing anything but aspens, however, as he replied, "Didn't notice anyone but me and these two ponies, coming from Boulder to here. Thought we had these hills to ourselves until just now. Are you saying I'm wrong?"

The old-timer nodded soberly and told him, "I thought you might be together, and to tell the truth it scared the bejesus out of me and old Scotty."

He saw Longarm wasn't following his drift worth mention and went on to explain. "I saw those three in the open to my north. So I cut the other way and then, just at the tree line, I spied you coming in from my south. Didn't you know

86

there was two other riders tagging a furlong behind you?"

Longarm frowned thoughtfully and replied, "I do now. It's my own damn fault for not looking back more often, just because the Indians have been peaceable this summer, so far. What did these mysterious riders you spotted on my tail look like, pard?"

The sheepherder said, "For openers, they weren't Indians. Both were dressed about like them three cattlemen you just chased away. One had a dark hat crushed Colorado style, like your'n. The other had on a high-crowned Texican ten gallon and, oh, yeah, batwing chaps of pale buckskin, almost white. I mind wondering how come, in warm weather with so little brush to pop in these parts."

Longarm asked if they were talking about batwing chaps with three conchos and darker lettering down either flap. He wasn't surprised at all to hear that was about the size of it. He just couldn't figure the why of it, once he'd figured the who!

Chapter 7

It didn't take much time and distance for Longarm to decide they were good, if they were really trailing him. For it wasn't easy to trail a man over hill and dale through broken cover with him trying to spot you and all concerned on horseback.

As the afternoon wore on, he began to suspect that old sheepherder he'd met back yonder had been off by himself too long. If he'd seen those mysterious riders at all, it was still possible they'd been up to something innocent. And hell, there was no law saying nobody but a missing lover-boy could have on batwing chaps and a ten-gallon hat. The sort of asshole who wore chaps just for show was more likely than most to spring for a big Texas hat. If the two of 'em had in fact been headed the same way along the same trail, and noticed a fuss starting up just ahead of 'em, they'd have only been acting sensible if they'd ridden around wide. The slopes this far down from the main spine of the Front Range were about as gentle one place as another, and if there might be more second-growth timber and sticker bush away from this fool game trail, that was what chaps were for in the first damned place.

He and his two ponies topped yet another wooded rise, about two hours after parting with that old sheepherder with the vivid imagination. Longarm reined in the mare he was riding and announced, "Time to swap mounts again, mounts. You two ought to enjoy the redistribution of my big rump, and I'd sure find it interesting to pause up here in the swell shade of these quivering aspen for a good gaze back the way we've just come. For there's no way anyone else is about to ride across that mile-wide dip of stirrup-deep open range without us noticing."

But it didn't work, if anyone was really trailing him. As he took his own good time swapping saddles, the only movement to be seen on the open slopes to his south, if you wanted to count it at all, was the ripple of the grass stems in the gentle afternoon breeze hither and yon where the stems grew tallest.

Longarm made sure of his grip on the lead line, knowing Brandy was the most likely to balk, and swung himself aboard the paint as he announced, "We've got to come up with a better way, pards. If they're dogging us at all, they're too smart to dog us tight. They're keeping at least one tree betwixt them and us at all times. On the other hand, if they're spying on us from that pine ridge across the way, what are we waiting for? Let's get on across the next open ground Cavalry-style, Powder River and let her buck!"

Neither pony had anything to say about it, of course, but the mare packing his lighter supplies fought the lead line like a sunfish, mighty vexed to discover there'd been a catch to that swell work as Longarm tore down the slope and up the next rise at a lope.

Not looking back, he rode over the next timbered ridge and down the far slope a piece before reining in and dropping to the deeply shaded forest duff with reins and lead line in one hand and his Winchester in the other. He quickly tethered both ponies to a sapling as he assured them he'd be back directly, Lord willing and the creeks didn't rise. Then he legged it back up to the shaded crest, dropping to one hand and his knees to ease up the last few yards and peer south across the open ground he'd just covered at a lope. A million years went by, and all that seemed to be happening was that the afternoon shadows were spreading wider, inch by inch, as the sun sank ever lower above the higher peaks to his west.

A gray jay fluttered down from the aspen canopy above to pace up and down in front of Longarm, cocking its small crested head to look him over with one little beady eye and then the other. Gray jays were like that. Longarm murmured to it, "I know how dumb I look to you right now, bird. It remains to be seen whether I'm at least as smart as your average Indian or all het up by an old sheepherder's hallucination. Ain't uncertainty a bitch?"

The gray jay fluttered closer with a sort of mocking caw, and landed on the barrel of the prone deputy's cocked Winchester, as if there weren't a better branch to preen on in the entire length of the Front Range. Longarm chuckled and told it, "Go ahead and smooth your fool feathers, but don't take too long at it, bird. I'm only fixing to give that sheepherder's haunts a few more minutes here."

The bird responded to Longarm's soothing human sounds with a sort of questioning caw. Longarm explained, "I learned to lay low like this in a war, one time. The trick is to wait the other cuss out and then wait him out just another damned minute. The one who gives his own position away first is inclined to be the loser."

He wondered if he'd spook the gray jay if he reached for an unlit cheroot to just sort of suck on, decided the perky little sass was more amusing than the risk was worth, and softly continued. "There have to be some limits to the time you expend on the game, of course. Nobody would never move and your average war would last forever if each side refused to move at all before the other did. You see, bird, a man in my position has to consider the possibility that there's just nobody there at all. Ain't you glad you ain't me? I could fuck up by moving on one infernal minute too soon, or I could fuck up by wasting Lord knows how many more fool minutes on nothing at all!"

The bird flicked its tail feathers at him, took a little crap, and wiped its feathery ass with its wicked little beak. So Longarm muttered, "Yeah, you're likely right. I've given the old man's spooks time enough, so shit on 'em."

Then something flashed brightly at him from the quivering aspens across the wide grassy swale, as if the low afternoon sun had bounced back from the east off a looking glass, or mayhaps a German silver concho. Longarm swore softly and booted the gray jay in the ass with his gun barrel, saying, "Get out of my damn sights, bird. There really is somebody over yonder and, damn it, how did they ever spot me over here after all the trouble I took to fox my backtrail?"

The bird had no advice to offer, having flown off, cussing him in its own harsh lingo. Longarm soon missed its company. For not another fool thing took place to distract him as the sun sank ever lower and, down the slope behind him, one of his ponies pawed the ground and called out in a worried whinny.

That, like the mysterious flash across the way, could be read more ways than one by a man who'd stayed alive up to now by reading things right, or if not right, mighty careful.

Crawfishing backwards through the trees on his belly until he knew he was safe from observation from that other tree line to the south, Longarm rolled to his feet and eased down to where he'd left his ponies tethered. He did so with his eyes peeled and his cocked Winchester's muzzle sweeping the cover all about in concert with his eyes. For spotting something and having to swing your muzzle to cover it could be a dead giveaway, and what you'd spotted might fire first in that case.

But Brandy hadn't fussed to tell him the one in the Colorado hat had circled wide while he'd been watching the other one flash his fool conchos across the way. Being a livery nag, Brandy was likely used to being fed and watered about this time of day, since most folks who hired a mount to ride had ridden enough by four or five, and since stable hands knew they had to feed and water all the stock before they had their own six o'clock supper. But as he untethered them both Longarm growled, "It's early and we could be in trouble. *I* could leastways. The two of you have been watered every damned time we crossed a fool creek up here today, and if you haven't had enough green clover and uncured grass to make you both sick as hell, tough shit. I'll see about your creature comforts once I know more about my own odds on making it to the South Saint Vrain alive and well."

He began to lead them along the ridge instead of over it, afoot. The paint didn't seem concerned about it. But Brandy commenced to roll her eyes at him the way some stock does when it's not used to watching humankind move about so short and stumpy-legged. Longarm gave her bit a good yank to show her just who was in charge of this damned expedition and told her, "I'm out to confuse them, not you. At least one of 'em knows it's easier to spot others on the skyline as the sun sinks lower. I just now proved that. I still don't know their final plans for us. But if they mean to move in on us ugly, I suspect they're waiting for darkness to fall. They're not too worried about losing sight of us as the sun goes down because they're figuring on me building a night fire for them to circle in on like a pair of murderous moths."

He led his ponies through some thicker second growth, ever farther from the trail, as he added, "They don't know me as well as you two. We'll just mosey along this ridge till we come to a better place to make a stand. Then I'll hide you both good, backtrack, and build that fire for them to circle in on. Only that won't be me they think they see bedded down by that fire. I might be slow, but I ain't stupid."

• • •

It didn't work. Longarm was sore as hell the next morning, after a nearly sleepless night and all the ingenuity he'd wasted on that son-of-a-bitching sheepherder's dire warnings.

He'd had no trouble finding a swell place to set up his ambush. For granite outcrops sprouted all along that ridge like big old heads of petrified cauliflower, rising church-steeple high above the treetops. So he'd selected one that was sort of hollowed out on top, the way lots of granite knolls grew, and hidden his stock up yonder before he'd improvised a decoy campsite with his hat and piled pine needles sleeping under a spare blanket against his McClellan and a sweet little night fire shedding just enough ruby light as the coals died down to encourage any murderous intent anyone for miles might have.

Then he'd stationed himself in a rock cleft above, with a clear field of fire and his Winchester across his drawn-up knees. Before midnight he'd needed another blanket wrapped around his shivering shoulders like a shawl, and by one or two A.M., the damned fire having gone out entirely, he'd caught himself dozing, gone down to throw more wind-fall on the damned fire, and wasted another couple of hours watching that one slowly flicker out, without attracting so much as a pack rat, as far as he could make out in the tricky gloom.

Then it had been morning. He'd rekindled the damned fire to fix himself some damned breakfast and a heap of black coffee before riding on, mighty disgusted. The old sheepherder might or might not have seen what he'd said he'd seen. Longarm had seen that bright flash from across the way, a hell of a long way. What he'd seen flashing was still up for grabs. Riding Brandy again, he moved down off that ridge at a sneaky angle in the gray mountain mists of morning, and took his own sweet time working them back to that trail this time. He paused here and he paused there, and if there was anyone following him now, the rascal had

93

to be made out of mist as well. For the morning sun shone through the trees of the ridges behind him, outlining them as if through the teeth of currycombs against the frosted skylight of a steamy bathhouse and, damn it, there just wasn't anybody back there.

If there ever had been, they'd gotten weary with whatever kid game they might have been playing. Longarm lit a fresh cheroot, broke the match stem to make sure it was all the way out, and confided to his mount, "I used to do fool things like that when I was a kid. I mind this one time me and some other third-graders from back home followed this old maid all the way to town and back, a good four miles through the West-by-God-Virginia woods, just to find out if it was true she had a secret lover she was screwing deep amid the blackberry bushes like some said. Only she didn't seem to be, the eight or ten times we trailed after her, creeping like fool Shawnee on our bellies, through the creeper vines and sticker bushes whilst she just walked to the fool notions store in town and back, along the fool road like a human being."

He took a deep drag, let it out, and decided, "That works. Say a couple of curious hands noticed us having that discussion with those Lazy H Bar Z riders. Say they tagged along a ways, noticed me staring back at 'em with a loaded carbine in my hands, and decided they'd have time to wash for supper if they headed home directly."

He still kept an eye on his back trail as the game trail carried him ever higher to the northwest. As he rode through ever more fir and far less aspen, he concluded this could be too much of a good thing if he ever meant to see Lyons at all. He'd aimed to circle in a mite wide, not wind up in Hot Sulphur Springs or some other such town on the far side of the Divide. So when they came to a fork in the trail he took the one to his right, knowing it had to lead at least a mite less high than the fork to his left. At the next point of vantage he reined in, well shaded by the dark firs brooding along that particular rise, and had a good long look-see, back the way he'd just ridden.

He lit a cheroot and smoked it most of the way down up there before he decided anyone tailing him, so far, had to be tailing so far back they'd just have to guess at which fork he'd just picked. He rode on, trending more to true north, and when he came to yet another fork, in a deep tangle of second growth, he again chose the one to his right, and hence more likely to trend downhill towards Lyons. The survey map he'd brought along in one saddlebag didn't show such small-scale features as single-file dirt trails through tick-infested tanglewood. But it was tough to get really lost in high country you'd been over before. To begin with, both the sun overhead and the general slope under him agreed which way lay east and west. So north and south had to fit crossways. He was able to judge how far north he was trending, at least where the trail rose high enough, by gazing about until he spied that familiar fool peak the boys liked to kid him about. The one old Dutch, in a burst of originality, had declared they'd named after U.S. Deputy Marshal Custis Long.

In point of fact, Long's Peak was named for another Long entirely. The bare triple-crested massif, still mostly white with snow this time of the year, had been discovered and climbed back in the early days of the beaver trade by Colonel Stephen H. Long of the U.S. Army Survey Service. Longarm had never met old Steve. But he had gone up the same mountain after outlaws one time, and concluded anyone who'd climb that high, especially along the scary trail up the eastern face, just for the hell of it, had to be *loco en la cabeza*.

Long's Peak rose exactly northwest of Boulder and almost due west of Lyons. So Longarm knew as long as he didn't overshoot such an obvious landmark, he didn't have to worry about winding up in, say, Larimer County by mistake. He knew he was supposed to hit the South Saint Vrain River just before he worked Long's Peak due west of him. The brawling "river," which would have been considered a glorified trout stream in wetter parts of the country, was born of the combined efforts of many a lesser mountain brook to combine into enough white water to get itself on the map at a point about a dozen miles east and a tad south of Long's Peak. From there the South Saint Vrain made a big jagged-ass curve to the north to swing down through Lyons, a half dozen miles and a whole lot lower to the east. Knowing all this, Longarm reined in when the trail cut across a fetlock-deep brook of bubbling snowmelt. As he let both ponies drink from it he reflected it just wasn't impressive enough to be the South Saint Vrain. But on the other hand, all that water his ponies were letting past their wet velvet muzzles had to be going somewhere, and there was a sort of rabbit trail following the bitty brook on the far side. So once he'd refilled his canteens from the cooler and fresher stream, he decided to follow it.

At the first serious bend he reined in, dismounted, and backtracked to see what sort of a trail he was leaving for anyone curious enough to care. The soil was gritty ground-granite that didn't hold hoofprints well. Once he'd cut a switch of fir and used it as a sort of broom to where he'd left the main trail and back, there were none at all. So he changed saddles and rode on aboard the paint.

A furlong or more downstream the water ran over a modest cliff. So the trail had to part company with the brook for a spell. But he could tell from the sounds of splashing and an occasional glimpse of sunlit water through the trees to his right that the narrow trail they were following ran more or less the same way, to hopefully meet up with the main stream further along where they'd know more about it— as the old Calvinist hymn would have it.

They were forging through second-growth cedar when he was suddenly glad he was riding the steadier paint gelding. Brandy would have surely spooked, and even the older cow pony tossed his head and bitched a mite when they came upon the line of spanking-new and needle-sharp bobwire some stupid greenhorn had strung through the thick growth, using the trunks of runty red cedars instead of regular fence posts, which would have been hostile enough, strung smack across the only trail as far as Longarm could see. He swore softly and declared, "A rider hitting this shit in the dark could work hisself into a killing rage, if he lived through the first surprise."

He dismounted. Had he had a pair of wire-cutters along he'd have simply cut the damned fence. For that was the unwritten law regarding such asshole disregard for established Western customs. Everyone knew a man had the right to fence in his own spread, whether his neighbors approved or not. Running a fence line across a public right of way, which an established trail was, no matter what your damned land deed might say, was just begging for a blood feud.

But seeing he didn't live around these parts and had other rows to hoe for Uncle Sam, Longarm led his ponies toward the stream along the fence line, on foot, in hopes there was a friendlier way to get through than by simply prying some staples out of some trees and stomping the sagging results into the dirt.

There was. The enthusiastic wire-stringer had stretched three strands above the running water, as if in fear a cow or mayhaps a trout might get away upstream. But there was yet another trail following the far side of the stream, this far down, and on that side it led through a gap in the wire, over a cattle guard.

So Longarm remounted, lest he wet his socks, and forded the ankle-deep ice water. He had to dismount again to haul both ponies across the cattle guard. You could do that with ponies. No cow would let you punch it through unless you stretched some planks for it to tiptoe along. So it had gates beat, in daylight. But as he eased the ponies through he agreed, soberly, "This would be another son of a bitch to meet up with blind after sundown."

The most popular form of cattle guard, as this one was, consisted of little more than a low spot scooped out of the dirt where the path cut through the fence line. Alone, that wouldn't stop livestock, even filled with rainwater after a shower. But once you laid six or eight logs in the shallow pit, crosswise, it was a bitch to get any hooved critter to even attempt a stroll across such ominous-looking footing. A human being, or a horse with human help and encouragement, naturally had no trouble simply stepping on the solid ground between the logs, if not the logs themselves, as boys and dogs preferred. Brandy put up the most fuss. Nonetheless, Longarm was soon mounted up and on his way again on the south side of the stream, for now. He began to see why as the way ahead opened up much more. The woods clung close to the running water on the far side of the brook. On his side the secluded mountain glen seemed flatter and more open. The grama and fescue all around were still fairly green and hadn't been grazed too heavy this year, so far. Then he spied a good-sized clump of larkspur and muttered, "Oh, shit, I might have known a nester who strung wire so carefree would let larkspur grow tall enough to flower, for Pete's sake!"

More likely to be called delphinium by gardeners back East, or even out West if they didn't keep livestock, the lovely but lethal larkspur sprouted stirrup-high flower spikes, lavender blue in these parts, and lacy green leaves that did awful things to any cows unwise enough to eat them.

Some held sheep and horses were affected less by the poison, while others pointed out that sheep, horses, and older cows seemed to avoid the stuff. Longarm didn't know what larkspur tasted like. He didn't care to find out. He assumed some cows got older by not liking the taste too much. All too many calves and yearlings did. He'd seen whole herds dead and bloated across grazing land badly infested with the poisonous shit. So when he met up with a half-dozen head of calico beef stock a quarter mile ahead, he rose in his stirrups, took off his hat, and commenced to slap it at them, yelling, "Git along down the mountain, cows. If this larkspur up this way don't kill you, I will. Move it, you rawboned scrubs fit for nothing but soup bones and glue, if that!"

They moved. Brandy, on her long lead, recalled she'd once been a cow pony too, and swung out to one side, unbidden, to shake her head like a big dog and stamp her front hooves like a spoiled brat when a chongo yearling tried to cut around them on that side. As they pushed the herd down the valley ahead of them, it grew. So did way more larkspur than any nester with a lick of sense would have allowed. So Longarm wasn't surprised when they passed one dead calf half damming the stream to his left with its bloated body. He spied three more, mostly among the trees out to either side, but allowed that wasn't too bad, when one considered how many pretty purple flowers he saw scattered all about. He'd gathered together a little over three dozen calicos, mostly longhorn and white-face crosses, when he spied the home spread they had to go with, a furlong ahead as they rounded a gentle turn to the southeast.

The main cabin and outbuildings had been fashioned of mostly fir logs, not yet seasoned as silver as they'd get by the time they'd stood up to a few short seasons of sun, wind, and moisture at this altitude. The wire back yonder had looked fresh too. There was a modest remuda of half a dozen ponies in one of the corrals. Longarm had the bigger one between the cabin and bigger log barn in mind as he drove the endangered cows on. The lady of the house must not have savvied what in thunder he had in mind. For she popped out a side door like an armed and dangerous cuckoo bird, waving the ten-gauge in her dainty hands as she bawled out, "Have you been drinking or are you out of your mind entire, cowboy? Those are my cows I see you pushing to perdition in broad-ass daylight and you'd best just cut that out this instant, if you don't want to catch a fistful of number-nine buck with your stupid grinning face!"

Longarm reined in, but went on grinning as he called back, "I ain't no cowboy, ma'am. I'm the law, only that ain't what inspires this mission of mercy neither. Why don't you open yonder corral and help me get your stock in alive before we discuss who might be stupid around here."

Chapter 8

She looked mighty puzzled. But as that same chongo tried to slip around the far side of *her* she raised both arms, shotgun and all, to shoo it back. Then she ran over to the corral, laid her gun aside, and opened the gate, even as she called out, "You'd better have a damned good explanation for all this bullshit, mister!"

Longarm was too busy to answer for the next few minutes. He had to let go the lead and do some cutting back and forth indeed on the paint to get the sassy-mouthed gal's herd in the corral. He'd have had an even tougher time if she hadn't helped on foot, waving the hem of her blue print dress at them and cussing like a mule skinner with a heavy load to haul over the hill.

At last they had all but one yearling in the corral. That one had dropped to the dust on its belly, like an overgrown yard dog, and when the gal tried to get it back up and on its way, showing a lot of bare leg in the process, the poor dumb brute just rolled its big sad eyes at her. So Longarm called out, "It's larkspurred, ma'am. Hold the gate just ajar and I'll see what can be done for it."

Suiting actions to his words, Longarm rode back to regather the cordovan packing his supplies, dismounted closer to the corral, and tethered both ponies to the same post before he strode over to the downed yearling, taking his pocketknife out.

The woman called, "What are you aiming to do with that blade? The critter don't look bloated."

He called back, "I just said he wasn't, ma'am. He's been eating larkspur. It does something funny to their blood pressure. Makes 'em feel like they're drunk and having a heart attack at the same time."

He strode around to the poisoned critter's rump, bent over to grab its tail, and hauled up hard with one hand as he cut the tail to the bone with the other. Knowing what to expect, he only got a few drops of blood on one boot tip as he sidestepped the gush and hauled the bawling yearling to its unsteady feet by the tail while the watching woman protested, "That looks mighty ugly, mister! Is that any way to treat a poor brute you just now diagnosed as sick?"

As he booted the wobbly yearling into an unsteady run at the corral gate, forcing the woman to sidestep in alarm, he explained, "It's the only treatment I know, this side of a vet with a medicine chest, ma'am. I can't say for certain that I saved the poor poisoned brute with that rough surgery. I do know that if they're down you got to get 'em back up *poco tiempo,* and the bleeding seems to help as well. The idea is to let 'em spill some extra blood pressure on the ground instead of inside 'em, through a busted blood vessel, see?"

She shut the gate, murmuring, "If you say so," in an undecided voice. He'd been able to see at a distance that she was built like a well-known brick edifice. This close, she was turning out pretty-faced as well. He figured her for, say, twenty-five to thirty, with big worried eyes the shade of horse chestnuts and light brown hair she wore close to her fine-boned skull, in tight braids wrapped over on the top of her head like a soft tiara. He wondered what she'd look like with her hair down, out of that loose-fitting gingham. He wondered why he was wondering anything that dumb, having wasted this much of a working day already.

He glanced at the sky, saw the sun was still high but shining sort of ashen through a fairly solid looking overcast and said, "Well, I've done about all I can for you folk, ma'am. When your man or menfolk get back from wherever they went, you'd best tell 'em there's way more larkspur on your land than the Lord ever meant cows to graze on. You do know what larkspur looks like, don't you?"

She soberly shook her pretty little head and said, "You keep saying larkspur and I still don't know what on earth you're talking about. As to my menfolk, I don't have any, no more. I've been a grass widow since last fall when a certain party who shall be nameless was inspired by hard cider at a harvest dance in Lyons to strike a woman in public, just for telling him he'd had enough."

Since *grass widow* was the country way of describing a divorcée, he felt there was no need to ask what she'd done about a man she'd just described as a drunken wife-beater. But she must have been sort of proud of herself. For she told Longarm, "After he got out of the hospital we agreed this spread was mine, free and clear. In return I split what we had in the bank with him, and if I never hear another word of him again it'll still be way too soon. I swear I must have been out of my mind to marry up with such an asshole and go way out west with him to raise cows and . . . Larkspur, you call that shit?"

He rolled his eyes heavenward, muttered, "Why me, Lord?" and asked her just how many acres overgrown with poisonous weeds they might be talking about. She swept one arm expansively to the east, saying, "I've got the bottomland between the barn and my main gate drilled to barley. Had some neighbor boys plow that forty for me just a few weeks ago and so the stock's not allowed down that way. If you came through my cattle guard, upstream, you've seen all my grassland. It's still mostly wooded, but

102

I reckon I'm grazing fifty or sixty acres, right?"

He grimaced and said, "More like eighty. By the end of July you'd have noticed you have it a mite overstocked, if your cows were still alive. They're sure to get into that larkspur, no matter what it may taste like, once they've grazed the sweeter grama and fescue short. They've already cleaned out any clover you might have started out with this spring."

She nodded and said, "I've been planning to sell off half the herd, the way prices have been rising in town this season. What can I do about this larkspur shit in the meantime?"

He sighed and said, "For openers, it helps a heap if you know what it looks like. So all right, do you have an infernal hay mower or at least a scythe around here anywheres?"

She said she had more than one scythe. So it could have been worse. They took his ponies over to her barn, where they got to relax with cracked corn and all the water they might want while Longarm removed his coat, rolled up his sleeves, and strode out to do battle with her scattered clumps of larkspur, scythe in hand.

She followed with her own scythe as he peered about for his first target. When she gleefully laid low some milkweed he warned her, "Don't waste sweat on butterfly fodder. I've only time to get you started. It's likely to take you all day and then some to take out all your larkspur, once you know what you're doing."

He spied a pretty plume of purple buds, just fixing to open, and pointed it out to her, saying, "That's larkspur."

He let her scythe it flat, close to the roots. As she did so she protested that it didn't look poisonous to her, dang it. He asked her what poison was supposed to look like, pointed out that oleander shrubs were even prettier, albeit twice as dangerous, and added, "Thank your stars oleander don't grow up here in the Front Range. It's becoming increasingly obvious, no offense, that you never grew up in these parts neither."

She admitted she was off a truck farm up the Hudson Valley from New York City. That led in turn to her sort of tedious life story as, together, they worked up the glen, scything larkspur every twenty to forty yards.

Her name, she said, was Catherine Block. She added that her friends made that Kitty. Block seemed to be the surname of the neighbor boy she'd married. They'd already established him as a wife-beating drunk who'd thought a family could make a living on a quarter section of marginal range, most of it overgrown with second-growth weed-trees and only about a third of it flat enough to plow. Longarm was too polite to offer uncalled-for discouragement. So he never told her that in his opinion the smartest thing she could do up here would be to sell out and go back East. He did explain, as they slowly worked their way up the narrow strip of open grazing, how most mountain outfits made out best by claiming a well-watered quarter section like this one, planting no more than a produce garden and orchard for their own private use, and stocking as many head as they could manage on surrounding open range. When she asked what she seemed to be doing wrong he told her, "Aside from allowing all this larkspur to creep in on you, there ain't much profit in barley unless you plant a heap of it, closer to market. Time you haul all you'll get off forty acres down to the breweries, closer to Denver, you'll do well to break even for your time and effort. As to your beef herd, ma'am, you just can't raise enough to show a decent profit on your own fenced-in grass."

She said, "We did back home in York State."

To which he wearily replied, "That's what I just said. You say you've been up this way at least since last year. So you must have gotten your small herd through one mountain winter and . . . "

"Last winter was unusual," she began.

It must not have cheered her much to hear him explain, "Last winter was one of the mildest on record, thanks to the drought last year. This summer the rainfall's turning out more normal, as you can see every time you look up this afternoon. If we're moving into the cooler and wetter part of the six- to ten-year cycle we seem to get out here, you can bank on at least one really deep freeze with, say, twelve feet of snow before this decade is out."

He saw he might have spooked her. So he said to soothe her, "Your notion of selling off your veal before the first frost is a good one. You'd do even better selling off your whole herd this fall and starting over next spring with fresh-bought calves. You just don't have the spread you need up here for anything but a marginal cattle operation. So why not settle for the most margin you can manage until you've the cash on hand to hire some hands and graze a real herd, serious, in the hills all around?"

She lopped some larkspur without answering. He said, "I didn't see any next-door neighbors riding down from the west. You still have plenty of open range around this one modest claim, right?"

She said, "I have. Only this one grassy glen is about all the decent grazing for many a country mile. Didn't you notice any trees at all as you were traipsing about up yonder?"

He nodded but insisted, "I just said raising beef in this high country was marginal. You can raise cows on cow pasture, the way they do back East, or you can let tougher Western breeds range farther and wider on marginal range, with enough hired help to keep 'em from wandering to ridiculous lengths, of course. There's a certain amount of orchard grass among all but the thickest timber. Cows and even ponies eat aspen leaves and bark when they're really hungry. So they tend to clear more range for grass as they struggle to survive in mixed stands. I could tell, riding in, these parts hadn't been settled as long as the country I just rode up out of. The Indians say that back in the Shining Times there was way more blue spruce and far less aspen in these hills. So in a way, you might say your cows have already started, up this way."

He felt something cold and wet hit his tanned bare wrist

105

as he scythed a good clump of larkspur. He glanced up at the gray sky and said, "It's fixing to rain fire and salt any time now, Miss Kitty. Don't you reckon we'd best head on back?"

She said, "Pooh, we're less than halfways to my back fence line, and you did say this was the only time you could spare me, didn't you?"

He replied that was about the size of it, but grudgingly moved on to destroy yet another clump of the innocent-looking evil as, off in the distance, the thunderbird flapped its big wings amid the churning clouds. The afternoon light was that funny shade where all the colors looked somehow more bright than they did in sunlight. The grass sparkled green as emeralds, and Kitty's blue and white print seemed fancy as blue-willow chinaware, while her soft brown hair had turned to taffy stretched ready to serve.

The oddly luminous light made it easier to spot the scattered spears of larkspur too, even as it warned of a pending electrical storm in the damned near future. So Longarm picked up the pace, sweeping his scythe wide and low, and if he took out a heap of grass as well, tough shit. When she commented on his draconian approach to weeding he told her, "Grass springs up as thick or thicker after it's et or mowed. Forbs and weeds like larkspur can't take near as much grazing. That's how come you see so few roses growing on a well-tended lawn. This larkspur may sprout back a time or two before it gives up the ghost. Now that you know what it looks like you ought to be able to keep ahead of it. If you don't let it flower and set seed *this* summer, you won't see near as much of it *next* summer."

They were close to that dead yearling bloating in the running water now. Kitty sniffed and said, "Oh, my God! I just took a sponge-off and made me some coffee with water I drew from this very creek!"

He shrugged and said, "It's ever safer to have a well so's you can pump all your water through a heap of clean deep dirt. I doubt you'd have to drill more than eight or ten feet, albeit I'd do so upslope from yonder surface water and well clear of any, ah, sanitary facilities out back."

She said she'd thought about that, only it was tough to improve a homestead when there were no men about the house. He smiled thinly and confided, "I simply don't have time to sink a well for you, even if I had the pipe and inclination. My boss would have a fit if he knew I was helping you out this much. I know it would be wrong to leave a lady and her cows in the condition I just found 'em in, but I was really sent up this way to hunt for outlaws, not mow meadows."

That naturally made her ask a heap of curious questions, and so he naturally filled her in on the curious case of Professor Jethro Markham and his college for crooks. She said she'd never in her born days heard a stranger story. He was too polite to tell her she should read more, or to ask if she could read. He asked some questions of his own, as long as he had the full attention of someone in those parts who might know.

She told him the bitty brook across her property did indeed run into the main channel of the South Saint Vrain, less than a mile northeast of her far line and main gate. She went on to assure him the wider wagon trace he'd be riding once he rode through that gate would take him and the South Saint Vrain on into Lyons, no more than a two or three hours' ride down the general grade. He told her he wanted to snoop around any abandoned cabins she might know about in those parts first. He explained, "I got just a few words about an old cabin along the South Saint Vrain out of a suspect before I left Denver."

She nodded, gracefully scythed another milkweed she mistook for larkspur, and said that made sense. To which he replied with a dubious frown, "Not to a master criminal, if that's what old Jethro's supposed to be. Everyone's been scouting high and low for a pretty slick crook called Jesse James, ever since most of his gang got rounded up at Northfield, back in '76. If there's a chicken coop or doghouse in the wooded hills of Missouri that ain't been scouted for our Jesse by now, it's a figment of someone's imagination. So I keep saying, if only I could get somebody to listen, that neither Frank nor Jesse James are going to be caught down any country hidey-hole because all such rustic hideouts have been scouted."

"Then you don't think they're ever going to catch those naughty James boys?" she inquired.

To which he replied with a disgusted grimace, "Oh, they'll be caught, if they don't die natural or get to shooting it out amongst themselves. But when we do find out where they've been hiding out all this time, I'll bet you anything it turns out they've been holed up smack in some town or mayhaps a big and innocent-looking farm just outside one. It ain't as if us lawmen don't know heaps of crooks live smack in town. It's just that nobody looks half as suspicious in or about a populated settlement as he does out in the middle of nowhere, haunting empty houses like a dumb old spook."

She said she understood, making her smarter than at least some of Professor Jethro's pupils. He asked if she or anyone she knew in that neck of the woods recalled any old cabins that might fit. She shook her head, nailed a real larkspur this time, and said, "Now that you've explained the needs as go with a good hideout, I suspect it would be mighty dumb to hole up in any of the half dozen old cabins I know of between here and Lyons, near the South Saint Vrain or back in the trees a mite."

He frowned thoughtfully and said, "Half a dozen is more than I bargained for, even on a longer and way sunnier afternoon than this. Let's stick to ones you know that might not be so visible from the riverside trail, for openers."

She pursed her lips and said, "Let's see, now . . . There's the Martin spread about a mile upslope on the far side of the river. Hank Martin thought he had a gold mine and let his woman and kids build the cabin whilst he dug pyrite, mica, or Lord only knows. That's about as remote a cabin

108

as I know, unless you want to count the Hamilton place. I understand it's just a shell, up near Signal Rock. I've never been there. They say the Kimaho Indians burnt the Hamiltons out, way back when."

He didn't answer as he scythed a really ominous clump of larkspur. The Kimaho Indians were as famous and as hard to pin down in this part of Colorado as those funny little geezers Rip Van Winkle got drunk with that time back in York State. The name meant something like friendly folk in Ute. Only no surviving Ute seemed to know beans about them, and Longarm had thought they were a purely imaginary tribe until he'd met two pretty little breeds, up on Long's Peak, who'd said they were part Kimaho as well as desperate for some screwing.

He warned himself not to think about screwing, damn it, and lopped off the biggest clump in sight as he told Kitty Block, "We've cleared the worse part of the stuff and it's fixing to come down any minute, ma'am."

She said, "Pooh, we're within sight of my back wire and I'd like to make sure of it all as long as we're way out here in any case."

Then a dazzling bolt from the still-dry sky sizzled down to reduce a blue spruce on the far side of the brook to toothpicks and swell-smelling smoke, making all the hairs on Longarm, at least, tingle mighty spooky. So when he saw her go right on scything he called out, "We've just time to make your side porch, if we run like hell, starting now."

She insisted they were almost done up there and added, "I doubt we'll make it anyways."

As if to prove her point another lightning bolt ripped the sky wide open, and they were both soaked to the skin by the time she could finish exclaiming, "See what I mean?"

So he laughed too, and seeing there was simply no way to get wetter, save by jumping in that babbling brook and lying facedown, he shrugged and moved upslope, toward her back fence, to demolish more larkspur as the thunderbird pissed all over the both of them.

At least it was a warm rain, for the Colorado high country. That was hardly to say they were enjoying a warm shower or even a tepid one with their damned duds on. He knew they'd both wind up chilled to the bone and courting galloping consumption if they didn't keep moving until there was some way to get way drier than this. He said so. She agreed, and they were hell on that larkspur as they worked on up to that bobwire in the deluge. When they'd seen about the last of it and she asked how much danger larkspur presented, mowed and tedded in the sun, he told her, "It'd be best to rake it, of course. But so far I've never seen a cattle outfit take the time and trouble. Cows ain't likely to mess with wilted funny-tasting hay as long as they have standing greenery to graze. By the time your herd'd scalped this limited range down to where they're really nosing for anything they can get at, the stuff we just cut should have lost its strength if it hasn't blown away entire."

She said she was glad, leaning on her scythe, with her wet brown hair running down like someone had poured maple syrup over her pretty skull, and both nipples showing through the sopping-wet gingham clinging to her shapely torso. It was funny how he'd failed to notice till now how Junoesque the strapping young Dutch gal had grown up to be on that farm in Rip Van Winkle country. It didn't have nearly the same effect on him as it had had on old Rip in that story. He felt wide awake indeed as lightning split yet another tree up a ways, and he suggested they get under some cover *poco tiempo,* lest they wind up fried as well as soaked.

She agreed, and said she'd race him back to her cabin. Then she lit out, laughing, before he could protest how dumb that sounded. He saw no sense at all in running through knee-deep wet grass, in a pouring rain, with his boots overflowing already, if getting there dry was supposed to be the object. So as she scampered down around the bend, her wet skirts hiked half up and clinging to her twinkling legs, he just ambled after her at a sensible steady pace, his clammy feet squishing in his soggy socks while rainwater cascaded off the brim of his wet Stetson. He knew he could likely smoke under the shelter of his broad hat brim, for that was one of the reasons J. B. Stetson of Philadelphia made hats with brims so wide. But Longarm knew that the cheroots in his vest pocket were only going to fall apart like fresh dog turds if he tried to handle them until they'd been dried out again.

The matches he was packing were waterproof, made down Mexico way with such events as this in mind. His derringer and sixgun were well oiled, and his spare .44–40 rounds were coated with a mixture of beeswax and tallow that would have kept a duck's ass dry in a sissy rain like this one.

He knew better than to take his billfold out and check its contents until he could do so under a roof, preferably near a stove. So there was nothing to do but keep walking. So he did. And though he soon lost sight of the running girl, he knew where she was going, if she had a lick of sense. He hoped she'd have the brains to have her stove lit by the time he caught up with her.

Chapter 9

He met some mighty soggy cows as he squished closer to her cabin. Some were already grazing the much safer grassland Longarm and their owner had just cleared. Most just stood there, shivering, to wait the storm out. Any Front Range cow old enough to butcher as beef knew how suddenly such noisy showers came and went.

As the cabin hove into view he saw Kitty had been smart enough to pick up her shotgun while she'd been opening the corral gate. There was no sign of her this side of the silvery veil of rainwater sheeting off the eaves of her side porch. But she'd have been stupid as hell if there had been. So he strode through the waterfall as well, there being no other way to get to her damned door, and when he tried the door latch he discovered it was unlocked. So he stomped his feet on the planking, polite, and strode on in.

He found Kitty Block on her knees by a cold stone fireplace, wrapped in a cream-colored Hudson Bay blanket like a half-drowned squaw. She smiled wanly up at him and said, "I'm having trouble getting these damned matches to strike,

112

and even when they do I can't seem to get this damned newspaper to burn!"

He squished over, taking out his box of wax-stemmed Mexican matches along the way, and hunkered down beside her, saying, "It's the altitude as much as the dampness. Takes less heat to boil water and more heat to set things on fire in this thin mountain air."

She giggled and said, "You're making a puddle under you I'd slap you with a newspaper for making if you were a puppy dog. I swear I think you got even wetter than me out there, strolling so casual in that tempest. You should have run for it, with me."

He got a Mex match going and held the bitty flame steady under a scrap of newsprint under some cedar shavings she'd shoved under more serious lengths of split aspen. As they waited for something more interesting to happen, he observed, "You got wet enough to need that blanket around you with nothing under it, didn't you?"

She clutched the cream wool more tightly around her, demanding, "Where does it show, you fresh thing?"

He smiled thinly and assured her, "It don't. But your feet are bare, if I read your wet footprints right, and that is your soaked-through gingham I see draped over that chair in yon corner, ain't it?"

She smiled sheepishly and said, "I see no lady's secrets are safe around a lawman like you. Would you like to get out of your own wet things and under a dry blanket? I've plenty more where this one came from."

He chuckled and resisted the impulse that first sprang to mind. It might have sounded clever to say he'd rather get under that blanket with her, but only boobs and idiots told females in advance that they wanted to get nekked with 'em. There was something in the union bylaws of the female species that required them to say no when a man just asked for it polite. So as the wax match stem burned way too close to his fingers and the damp newsprint slowly turned brown and just a mite smoky, he muttered, "After I get this fire lit, maybe. How come you've been splitting aspen to burn when you got all that standing evergreen wood to clear outside?"

She said she'd found aspen way easier to chop down and split. He saw one match wasn't going to do it, and stuck the head of a fresh one in the same place to burst into flame without giving away any edge to thin air and damp paper. He dropped the small waxen end of the used-up match on the paper to melt into it as he muttered, "Considering how hard it is to light any fool logwood on a day like this, aspen's hardly worth the bother. The reason it's so easy to take apart with an ax is that it's mostly air and water. If I were you I'd get in plenty of pine, spruce, and fir wood, with mayhaps a quarter cord of cedar for kindling before the nights get really cold again, come no later than September on this east-facing slope."

She sighed and said there was just more work than one poor woman alone could manage on this lonely little spread. He saw the paper he'd soaked with melted wax burst into wan flames at last, and told her, "I said before you'd do better selling off your beef and barley entire this fall and starting fresh, next greenup, with new seed and veal. You surely know there's little comfort and no profit at all to spending a good part of the winter snowed in and the rest of it with goose bumps."

She shuddered under her blanket and murmured, "Don't I ever know it! There were times, last January, when I swear I'd have taken my husband back if he'd shown up halfway sober and willing to let me warm my poor feet against his bare hide."

Longarm didn't answer. As he gingerly shifted some split cedar to catch the rising warmth of the smoldering newsprint, Kitty heaved a bitter little sigh and said, "Good Lord, listen to me run off at the mouth about such intimate matters! I must be coming down with cabin fever, the way they say old hermits get! To hear me go on like that, a body might think I was out to get fresh with a house-guest!"

Longarm reached for the pile of old newspapers to one side of the fireplace, and began to tear thin ribbons and twist them as he softly assured her, "You only sound a mite lonesome to me, Miss Kitty. I wish there was some way I could cut you a cord of decent firewood and even warm your feet, the way you say you like 'em warmed, but I told you before that I'm only passing through on serious business. I wouldn't have tarried half as long as I already have if it hadn't been for that larkspur and this gullywasher."

She shifted her squat a tad closer to his as she confided, "I'm glad it's raining so hard, and I hope it won't let up before sundown. You wouldn't be able to poke about those empty cabins between here and Lyons unless you had plenty of daylight left, right?"

He held a paper twist above the still-feeble flames, and noted with mild pleasure that this worked way cheaper and at least as good as his limited supply of Mex matches. He had some of the split cedar going now. Before it could go out he poked it farther back, and shifted a green-barked but quartered aspen log so its bare white sapwood and few inches of tea-stained heartwood were catching the little fire rising against the damned damp back-wall of the granite fireplace. He said, "There we go. If it goes out again we're going to have to try some coal oil. For I've done about all a mortal can hope to do with damp kindling and green aspen wood."

She nodded and said, "I've already noticed you were mighty handy at the usual chores of menfolk. So how's about it—are you fixing to ride on, cold and wet in the clammy aftermath of this storm, or would you just as soon spend the night here and start fresh in the morning with a whole dry day ahead of you?"

He shot a wary glance at the gray light peeping through the nearest small window at them, favored her with an uncertain smile, and said, "You'd slap my face if you knew how tempting that offer just sounded to me, Miss Kitty. Anyone can see this day's about shot, even if the rain lets up within the hour."

She cast a thoughtful glance at the roof beams above them and told him, "Judging from the way it's still drumming on my poor roof, I'd bet you most anything we're good for another hour's worth at the least. What were you doing to me in your naughty head that I ought to slap you for, ah, Custis?"

He laughed and said, "It don't rate a real slap unless I really do it. Since it's understood I'll be riding on to Lyons in the cold gray dawn of common sense, I'd best not do anything I'd deserve corporal punishment for. But to tell the truth, this bitty fire's not doing a thing for me, and as these wet duds dry on me they're commencing to feel cold as a banker's heart. So about that blanket, if your offer is still good . . ."

She rose gracefully to her feet, as he did the same, and told him, "I've plenty, stored in that big cedar chest at the foot of yonder bed."

So he followed her over to the handsome brass bedstead she had niched in one corner of the ample one-room cabin. As they got there she turned to face him with her bare feet on the braided rag rug in front of the bed thoughtfully added, "Of course, if you'd as soon share this blanket with me, I'm certain we'd wind up a heap warmer way faster."

He felt inclined to agree as she spread her bare arms to throw open her blanket like big creamy wings. For she had light brown hair all over, and her ample but slim-waisted nudity was unblemished and even more tempting than vanilla ice cream splashed with chocolate syrup. So he started to take her in his arms. But she protested he was still covered with all that itchy wet tweed, told him not to be so predictable, and threw herself down across her bed quilts, blanket and all.

This naturally inspired him to hang his hat and gun rig on the bedpost, let everything else fall to the braided rag rug, and fall down beside her, covered with goose bumps until he gathered her vanilla curves in his arms and hauled

116

in for that kiss at last. For even though she protested he felt cold as ice, she kissed back swell and her curvaceous body felt warm all over.

As he parted the thatch of the grass widow with his wayward organ-grinder, and heard her sob in mingled surprise and desire for more, he told himself not to tell her it was dumb to feel too serious about all this. He knew she was a smart as well as sex-starved gal of mature years and some experience. As he began to experience the great pelvic motions of a lady who'd obviously done this sort of thing before and liked it a lot, he began to feel less guilty about the inevitable way this would end. He still knew Billy Vail would have a fit if he ever found out his senior deputy had spent this much time and effort with otherwise innocent suspects when he was getting paid to track down men and treat 'em a hell of a heap meaner than this!

What Billy Vail didn't know couldn't hurt him, and what the two riders hunkered in a deserted cabin farther down the trail to Lyons didn't know was driving them loco as they stared out into the shifting silvery sheets of summer rain. They'd been afraid to even try to light a fire on the old mossy hearth, and the two ponies hiding under the leaky roof with them didn't give off half the heat the men could have used. As the one with his hat crushed Colorado-style tamped his damp boots on the dirt floor in a vain effort to warm his clammy feet, the one with his high-crowned ten-gallon creased more Panhandle told him, "That ain't going to work, and that son-of-a-bitching lawman ain't going to come this way at all, cuss his hide! What say we just pack in the grand notion of killing him here and kill him somewheres else, some other time, when our gun hands ain't so numb and stiff from the cold?"

The one with the more sensible hat on snorted in disgust and asked, "Why don't we just give up the notion entire, if I follow your drift all the way home like the little piggy run? We can't ride on till this rain lets up, lest we wind up even

117

colder and stiffer. That pesky lawman ain't come down yon trail for the same clammy reasons, you poor shit! What'll you bet he holed up, the same as us, when this mean weather caught him further up the trail?"

The one in the big hat, looking along the trail from the unglazed window opening cut through the dark damp logs, demanded, "Where, then? There ain't another deserted homestead like this one, this side of Lyons."

His companion snorted in sheer disgust and snapped, "Well, of course there ain't, you asshole! I suggested we ambush him here for that precise precious reason! When we lost his trail to the south, I told you he'd wind up on that one, out front, for the same reasons all roads leads to Rome. There ain't no better trail to Lyons from the higher ones we lost the son of a bitch on and there ain't a better ambush anywhere along it than this very cabin. So shut up, keep a sharp eye out for him, and let's just *git* the rascal, hear?"

That Scottish poet had been right about the best-laid plans of mice and men, even though Longarm didn't know about the two would-be bushwhackers shivering down the trail ahead as he rubbed his warm belly against Kitty's, their bare flesh almost too warm for comfort as his efforts in bed combined with those earlier ones in the fireplace to cheer the place up considerably.

During a trail break to catch up on their breathing, Kitty insisted on hanging his damp duds up to dry properly, lest he ride on into town looking rumpled enough to scare folk. So he smoked a half-dry cheroot, propped up on one elbow, and watched her sweet vanilla form move gracefully at her naked chores by the cheerful flickering firelight as, overhead, the rain began to ease off.

It had stopped entirely, save for an occasional frog-plop here and there, by the time she had all his stuff spread out to dry on the backs of chairs between them and the fire. She must have noticed how far off that last thunder had rolled, because she said with a sigh, coming back to bed with him, "It's dark out now, dear. You'd never be able to see a thing along the trail now, whether you've had your fill of me or not."

He had, in fact, fired quite a few salvoes into her sweet wet warmth, as any man in bed with such a pretty lady might have been expected to. He still gathered her in for a friendly kiss, holding his cheroot to one side as he held her tongue as tightly between his lips, and told her as soon as he was able that he hadn't had near as much of her as he felt up to, yet. She responded to his gallantry by grabbing his smoke and snuffing it out, even though there'd been plenty of puffs left, and then helping him feel up to it by puffing on him, with way more skill than your average willing schoolmarm might have managed.

He didn't ask where she'd learned to play the French horn so fine. She'd admitted she was a grass widow who'd thrown her man out for drinking too much and not screwing her too much—or even enough, most likely. The nice thing about bedding a widow, with her husband missing above or below the grass, was that you didn't have to talk them into half the things unwed women never allowed they knew about, no matter how many others they'd already "lost their heads" with. That was what gals liked to call screwing, until they'd done it often enough legally, to admit they weren't virgins or, at the most, recently raped schoolgirls. He chuckled fondly down at the part in Kitty's soft brown hair as her head bobbed up and down so naturally. She heard him, and raised her face from exactly where he wanted it to frown up at his, asking what was so funny about the way she spoke French. He assured her he'd just been reminded about something old Ben Franklin had written about women. It would have been rude to add that Franklin had advised young men who really wanted a good time to stick with older women. She dimpled sweetly, said she'd heard tell Doctor Franklin had spent a heap of time in France, and would have gone on the same sweet way had he not warned her, "Waste not,

119

want not!" and hauled her bare belly up his to sort of haul her on the great erection she'd inspired as if her sheath had been tailor-made to fit his weapon.

She gasped, "Oh, yesss! I just love it when a gentleman rises to greet a lady! But let me get my heels into your armpits so's we can work it even deeper, darling!"

He was willing to try anything that didn't hurt. But in the end they naturally finished with him on top and her bare heels drumming on his naked shoulders. Being inconsiderate as most women, once they've had their way with a man, she told him he was in too deep once she'd come herself. So he finished dog-style, which as any old married couple can tell you is unromantic but comfortable enough to just go on screwing and chatting indefinitely.

He assumed she hadn't always been sore at her ex-husband when, as expected, she fell into a relaxed conversation with him as he stood there barefoot on the braided rug with her shapely bare behind thrust up at a comfortable angle for both of them. He felt it was only his duty to find out as much as she might know about surrounding landmarks and such neighbors as might go with them. She'd already told him about that empty cabin over by the river, and since he had no way of knowing a couple of jaspers were laying for him there he pressed her, as he humped her, for more details about any recent arrivals in those parts.

She confessed that as far as she knew she and her ex-husband had moved in after most every other neighbor she knew to howdy. As he prodded his own memory as well as her, he described Professor Jethro Markham as well as he could picture the mysterious cuss himself. When she allowed there seemed to be scads of middle-aged gents with salt and pepper hair and blue eyes in those parts, he insisted, "Study on an otherwise nondescript older gent a tad taller and more lantern-jawed than average, with the colors of the Confederacy tattooed on, let's see, I think it was his left shoulder."

120

She giggled and wiggled her rump at him as he slid in and out of her. She said, "Heavens, Custis, I don't invite old gray-haired men to take off their duds in my company. Only the young good-looking ones I can catch. A Confederate flag, you say?"

Longarm got a better grip on her hip bones to keep it in good as he mused half to himself, a mite distracted, "Yeah, the Stars and Bars on a sort of shield instead of a square flag, though. Markham rode with guerrilla raiders instead of the regular army of the South, way back when. That's likely what made him act so proud about it. A heap of the more famous Southern officers were dressed sort of raggedy near the end, yet they say the glorified bandit Quantrill was gussied up like Robert E. Lee that time he burnt out Lawrence, Kansas, whilst Lee and the real Southern army was fighting way closer to Gettysburg."

She said she'd had an older brother killed at Gettysburg with some other old boys of the New York 69th. When she asked him if he'd been in the war he grunted, "Yep. I forget the number of my regiment, and we were talking about a guerrilla raider who thinks he knows enough about train robbing to give classes on the subject. You'd have heard if there was a sort of trade school in these parts, say, classes in punching cows or prospecting, as far as the neighbors were supposed to know?"

She arched her spine and purred, "Oh, yes, that feels just right." She added, "I reckon I'd have heard if there was any school at all—outside the city limits of Lyons, that is. I asked about that when we first come out from York State. That was before I decided never to have any children with that no-good drunk I came out with—or anyone else, thank you just the same."

It was starting to feel just right to him as well, as she went on, breathing faster. "There's more than one grade school in Lyons and, let's see, I think they said there was a little red grade school up the post road to Estes Crossing, even farther from here than Lyons."

He humped her harder, saying, "I'm talking about a more private sort of school, for older kids, and let's turn you over and finish this right, little darling!"

She was more than willing, and later, as they lay sleepy-eyed in one another's arms, he gave up on pumping her about local mysteries. For as luck would have it, he'd wound up in bed with a gal who, for all her good points, didn't really seem to know those parts as well as he did. When they woke up hungry, along about ten, he had to build the fire in the stove for her to brew them some hot chocolate and heat up some stew she'd made earlier. When he noticed the stew meat was elk and commented on it, she said a hand off a neighboring spread had let her have an elk haunch for some of her sourdough bread. He didn't ask what that other cuss looked like, and when she fixed him up with some sourdough, sweet butter, and elderberry preserves for dessert, he was more inclined to believe she might have gotten her stew meat innocently.

Thanks to her serving sensible hot chocolate instead of coffee at that hour, they both got to sleep a good six or eight hours, and by the time he'd screwed them both wide awake and she'd fixed a swell breakfast for them, with strong black coffee this time, the sun was shining fit to bust outside. So they washed up, got dressed, and reluctantly parted about the time he usually got to the office down in Denver.

That left him less of the morning than Billy Vail might have approved of. But it was still fairly early after noon when Longarm rode into Lyons at last, having poked about more old abandoned cabins—and been coffeed and caked at the occupied ones—than he'd planned on to begin with.

Save for that one empty cabin near the river, closest to town, he'd found no sign anyone else had seen fit to visit any of the empty ones within a morning's ride west of town. That still left downstream, east of town, unless those fresh horse apples and boot-heel marks he'd spied in that one old tumbledown cabin meant anything.

Near the center of Lyons he dismounted out front of the Peakview Livery, and bet the young breed in the doorway two bits that they'd be unable to find two stalls and some oats for his ponies. The kid said he'd lost, but charged him an extra dime to store his McClellan and possibles in their tack shed.

Longarm was starting to feel hungry again, maybe because all the recent fresh air and exercise had given him an appetite. But thanks to the swell flapjacks Kitty had made right after she'd made love to him that last time, he was able to hold out as he passed the open doorway of a tempting chili parlor, for now. He'd have been less able to if he hadn't spied the black and yellow sign of a Western Union office just beyond.

The clerk inside was female, a pleasingly plump strawberry blonde with pencils stuck in the bun she'd built like a bird's nest atop her pretty little head. When he told her who he was and what he wanted, from Western Union leastways, she looked impressed and told him she had messages indeed for him if he was the notorious Longarm.

He smiled modestly down at her to assure her, "Heck, I ain't so notorious, ma'am. Just a mite famous, is all. Could I see them wires now?"

She handed them over, flustered and blushing for some fool reason. He was just as glad he'd torn off that last piece with old Kitty that morning. Pretty little gals that blushed and jiggled like this one could distract the hell out of a man when he was hard up and not determined to damn it do his duty around there, whatever that might be.

One message he tore open was from Iowa, assuring him anyone intimating their state prison had discharged Jethro Markham under the mistaken impression he was Hiram Paget had to be mixing his opium with locoweed because the late Jethro Markham was damn it buried out back and they were sending rogues' gallery photographs of both the silly sons of bitches to Denver, not there, because Henry had made Western Union forward the wire from Iowa and they likely had no notion where he really was.

He folded the self-serving wire neatly and put it in a side pocket of his frock coat for now. He'd have been way more surprised if the prison officials who'd surely let *somebody* out had agreed they'd made an almost impossibly dumb mistake.

Billy Vail had wired, personally, that on further reflection and full of painkiller, the wounded outlaw who'd just lost a flipper at County General under the name of Festus Larkin had allowed he might have been born Festus Wade and that the so-called Wade boys might have started out under the name of Warring. On further questioning he'd suggested the late Rafe Wade, his brother, had gunned, true enough, had really started out as Jimbo Downey, while Lem Wade had been neither a Lem, a Wade nor any blood kin to anyone in the gang. The very sick and heavily sedated young outlaw had agreed he found all those made-up names confusing himself, and explained the professor had told them that was the whole point. Billy Vail said he had no idea where Markham had come up with Lem or Rafe to begin with. Longarm put that wire away, picked up a pencil, tore off a telegram blank, and proceeded to tell his boss about the missing Raphael Farnsworth, leaving out the sassy parts about his big sister, Judith. He added that it was up for grabs whether her baby brother had run off to join a gang of budding train robbers or whether they'd robbed him and tossed him down some mine shaft, there being more of *them* than new trade schools in these parts, as far as he could see.

When he'd finished, he handed it to the plump but pretty blonde, but told her, "This can wait for now, since it's not half as informative as I'd like. You being the one who'd transmit most important messages in and out of Lyons, and me being a lawman seeking information on such matters, what say we put our heads together and see what we can figure out."

She made a little puckered asshole with her moist pink lips and said, "Ooh, I'm not allowed to discuss the messages of one client with another, sir!"

He said, "I'm not another client, I'm the law, and since you must have paid some attention to those wires I just got, whilst you were taking them down off the wire, you must know I'm up here on serious business after serious outlaws."

She gulped, said she'd noticed, but insisted, "I could wire company headquarters and ask their permission, if you like. But it could mean my job if they ever found out I'd passed on private messages. For they told me when I took this job that we were sworn to secrecy about such matters!"

He nodded, understandingly, and said, "I've had this same conversation before, and it'd sound like bragging if I told you how often I've lost. But let me rephrase things a mite, lest you mistake me for a needlessly nosey cuss. To begin with, there's no sense you wiring headquarters for that permit. I can tell you what they'll say and I don't have to know what anyone else has sent past you, in so many words. You could tell me if any of those many names you just took down for me were familiar to you, right?"

She nodded brightly and confided, "Nobody by any of those names has sent or received any messages across this very counter."

He smiled back and said, "*Bueno*. If there was a new school, or even a new business in town, started by strangers you'd never heard of before, you could tell me that much, couldn't you?"

She said she sure could, but added that there just weren't any new businesses in Lyons, unless he wanted to count a new hardware shop across from the livery. He said he'd noticed their sign looked fresh, doubted it meant much, and added, "Lyons sets at the west end of a railroad spur. You'd have heard if anyone around here had been robbing trains, wouldn't you?"

She dimpled up at him and replied, "Of course we would. Wouldn't you?"

To which he could only reply, morosely, "That's what I thought. In sum, I might have followed the last words of a dying outlaw all this way in vain. I'll be back if I come up with any sensible questions, ma'am."

She said her pals called her Billie and that she got off at six. He said he'd remember that and left to see if that chili joint still smelled as good.

Chapter 10

It did. But knowing he'd wasted way more time than he'd planned, and seeing he still had the usual courtesy call to pay on the local undersheriff and town law, he settled for no more than one bowl of chili with oyster crackers and two cups of coffee before he pushed away from the counter, paid off, and strode back out into the bright mountain sunlight, picking his teeth.

Coming the other way, as if to prove how grand that chili smelled, came a somewhat younger cowhand, sporting a tall Texas hat, batwing chaps, and a brace of ivory-gripped sixguns. His chinless face had worn a sort of sneaky expression even before he'd spied Longarm coming out the very door he'd been headed for. His shifty green eyes went even shiftier as they locked gazes, and then the penny dropped for the both of them. So they went for their guns, fair and square, and the rat-faced cuss with conchos flashing down those light tan chaps was good!

So good that he might have won if Longarm hadn't noticed, just in time, how the darker leather lettering applied to those flappy chaps had been ripped off, recent, as if to hide the way they'd been initialed or branded to begin with.

It was still was closer than Longarm would like to think about for at least a few nights to follow. The sneaky rascal beat Longarm to the draw by mayhaps a full split second. After that, the double action of Longarm's more modern Colt .44−40 Model T shifted the odds a tad in the name of the law. Longarm's sixgun roared sooner and straighter. The stranger in the Texas hat still fired his own guns, both of them, into the dirt between them before he wound up spread-eagle in the street on the far side of all that dust and gunsmoke.

Longarm moved in fast to kick both fallen sixguns clear of his fallen foe, no matter how slack-jawed and starry-eyed the son of a bitch gazed upwards. Then, before he did another thing, Longarm got out his badge and pinned it to his left lapel, assuring the townsfolk who were all around, though hanging back a mite, "It's over and the right side won. I'm the law. I'm still working on who this other cuss might be."

As the gathering crowd edged somewhat closer, Longarm reached inside his coat for that sepia-tone with his free hand. He got it out, compared the two blurry faces in the photograph with the dead face framed by that big Texican hat brim, and muttered, "Aw, shit."

Then he put the sepia-tone away, reloaded, and holstered his .44−40 for now before he hunkered down to go gingerly through the duds the cuss had bled and shit in for the few seconds it had taken him to cease and desist his twitching. The three neatly spaced albeit still-smoking holes in his shirtfront had dealt him out of the game about as fast as possible, but it took the parts a man didn't think with a little more time to figure out they were dead too.

There was nothing in the way of I.D. aboard the corpse, unless you wanted to suspect a two-bit wallet with fourteen dollars in it meant something. The nickel mouth organ meant the cuss had likely played sad cattle songs somebody else might recall. The pocketknife said nothing, and the half-consumed plug of Rooster Brand chaw could have been bought at any general store in the country cheap.

Someone in the crowd called out, "It was a fair fight and the one as lived through it says he's a lawman too, Stump."

So Longarm was glad he'd put away his own gun and put on his own badge when he glanced up to see the Boulder County lawmen looming over him, wary-eyed but, so far, just resting their hands casual on their gun grips.

Rising back to his full height, and failing to see how the much shorter and older Boulder County rider could have been nicknamed more fittingly, Longarm said, "I'd be U.S. Deputy Marshal Custis Long. I don't know who I just shot it out with. We just met mighty informal. I thought for a moment I might have got my fool self involved in a love triangle. But the face don't match them batwing chaps and that ten-gallon hat as I feared, thank God."

A local man sporting a straw hat and butcher's apron edged in to declare, "I sold some sandwich meat to that one and a pal dressed more natural only this morning, Stump. They never said who they might be or who they might ride for. I can't say I took 'em for owlhoot riders, though, until just now."

Longarm asked the butcher to describe the dead man's sidekick better. The butcher shrugged and replied, "That one you just shot did all the talking. His pal stayed in the doorway with the brim of his Stetson shading his face pretty good. Oh, yeah, his hat was darker and crushed regular, Colorado-style. Does that help?"

Longarm started to get out that sepia-tone again, but decided not to bother. A witness who described foggy could give you the wrong mental image indeed.

The taller and younger of the two local lawmen had been studying the dead man's chaps. He said, "I read the stitch holes left when someone tore the applied cutouts off as a double L on his right wing and some kind of brand on the left, Stump."

The older lawman nodded soberly and declared more certainly, "So do I, and Diamond E fits that stitching good enough. This must be the missing rider the Lazy Four reported. I'd have to look it up. It's been a spell. But didn't Long Jim, the ramrod out to the Lazy Four, say the poor soul answered to Lucky something or other, Walt?"

Walt, if that was the younger one's name, replied, "Lucky Lem something Irish. But what's he doing dead on our street today if he's been missing all this time?"

Longarm said, "If we're talking about Lucky Lem Corrigan, from down by the county seat, this ain't him, and a lady who seemed mighty vexed with the real Lucky Lem might owe him an apology."

He went on to fill them in on the little he knew, leaving out some of the spicier details. He'd barely finished when Stump decided, flat out, "I know who you are now. You're the one they calls Longarm. Why didn't you say so? They wired us you might be up this way, only we'd about given up. That escaped lifer, Jethro Markham, never showed up in these parts, no matter what anyone else might have told you, so—"

"You know about Professor Markham and his odd views on education?" Longarm cut in. "How can you say for sure I'm on a snipe hunt? I just rode through a heap of mighty tall timber and I'm sure I missed a heap more than I ever saw."

Stump replied, a mite smugly in Longarm's opinion, "We know our own neck of the woods better, and me and Walt here ain't the only ones riding for Undersheriff Baker. There's *money* on the head of that there Jethro Markham. So you might say we've been scouting for him sort of inspired."

A tall drink of water in a rusty black suit and stovepipe hat joined them. When Stump introduced him as the Lyons undertaker with the best voting record, Longarm was just as glad the cuss didn't offer to shake. For he looked at least as dead as the gent on the ground, even if he could walk and talk a mite better. When he asked who he was supposed to bill for clearing the streets of Lyons and planting the results in potter's field, pine box five dollars extra, Longarm heaved a wistful sigh and said, "Me, care of my office in Denver, if I can't get the department to accept this as a proper business expense. But before we decide how to package him for burial, is there any way you can keep him above ground, for viewing, should we find anyone who might be able to I.D. the mysterious cuss?"

The undertaker bragged that he could keep anybody around, fresh as a daisy, or at least not too disgusting, for as long as the money kept coming. He explained, "You have to replenish the embalming fluid every few days, and of course they will turn that morose shade of liver gray on you if you don't apply heavier cosmetics as required."

Longarm grimaced and said, "I ain't about to pay for face powder for a dead man, damn it. I'm familiar with the funny colors we turn in the sweet by-and-by. It's the maggots and stink that makes it tough to study a dead face long enough to recall whether it's someone you used to know or not."

The undertaker looked almost as green as the two local lawmen as he assured Longarm he knew what was required and to just leave the trimmings to him.

So they did, and went across the street to inhale some needled beer in the handy saloon some angel of mercy had built there. Longarm put half his schooner of spiked suds away before he relaxed enough to light a cheroot and ask them to go back over that part about scouting the wooded hills all about for Professor Markham and his college of crime.

The local lawmen said almost all the settlers in those parts were well-known to them, leaving them only a few recent arrivals to sniff around. To test them he asked what they might know about a certain grass widow up the riverside trail a ways. In the end he doubted either Stump or his younger and prettier sidekick knew old Kitty as well as he did, but they had her story down pretty good. He was glad she hadn't lied to him about that no-good husband who'd broken her in so fine before she'd broken his jaw with a bentwood chair for raising his hand to a lady.

Walt said none of the few new hands on any of the surrounding spreads fit the description of the older escaped lifer or anyone else they had wanted flyers on. Stump said, "We backtracked a couple of the bigger talkers anyway, *por nada*. The report we got from your office the other day wasn't the first we'd heard of some asshole teaching outlaw skills, like that Fagin cuss in that book by Dickens. Some whores who double as informers told us about that bullshit."

"And?" Longarm asked with sudden interest.

"And it panned out bullshit, like I just said," the older local lawman replied. "I don't know why it is that some men can't screw a woman without bragging how ferocious they are. I've seldom met a woman who preferred a bad man over a sweeter talker with a steady job. But boys being boys, some of the cowboys have been telling the whores about this wise old bird who can take most anyone under his wing for a course in hotshot crime and graduate him in six weeks as too slick to sit on flypaper without sliding off."

Walt chimed in. "They say the course costs two hundred dollars, or almost six months' pay. What I can't figure is how come a man who knows so much about stealing and not getting caught would have to make money so tedious. I mean, if *I* knew how to get money without having to work or go to prison—"

"You're smarter than most of the folk who wind up in prison," Longarm cut in. "Markham wound up in prison his fool self when he tried to apply some of the criminal science he brags on knowing all about. How do I go about questioning those whores who picked up on the brag?"

Stump told him, soberly, "You don't. Not without clearing it with Undersheriff Baker, and I can tell you what he'd tell you to do to yourself, impossible as it sounds."

Walt explained in a kinder tone, "This is an election year, and how would it sound to our regular voters if we allowed whores to exist in Boulder County? We got in on the same reform slate as everyone else after the Grant machine had raped the whole country wide open."

Longarm grumbled, "Damn it, boys, I know the rules on dealing with shady informants, and it ain't as if I'm indiscreet. Half-cracked or not, Markham is dangerous! Sooner or later his pupils figure to kill again."

Stump shrugged and said, "The one you just shot it out with must not have done his homework." When Longarm pointed out the contest had been closer than he liked to think about, the older lawman relented enough to say, "We might be able to let you jaw with a more decent informant who ain't on our protected list. A squatter raising ponies a couple of miles down the river did report a mighty odd conversation with some strangers, now that I think back on it."

Walt brightened and said, "Why sure, Stump. I was there too when old Thorp Ralston dropped by to tell us about them young saddle tramps. But since we never caught up with neither, they must be long gone by this time."

Stump silenced his sidekick with a frown and told Longarm, "The old squatter told us these two kids rid in, around supper time, and offered him five hundred, between 'em, to show them the way, as they put it. Ralston said he'd show them anything but his asshole for five hundred dollars. Only then the conversation commenced to get sort of evasive, and they decided they might have stopped at the wrong address."

Longarm nodded and asked for directions to the address the two mysterious riders had apparently mistaken for another. Stump said, "Old Thorp Ralston's resettled the abandoned Whipple claim, down the South Saint Vrain a piece. We're ahead of you on that angle. Your boss wired us about that dying declaration about old cabins, and Thorp Ralston's about the same age as Jethro Markham."

Walt chimed in. "Came up from the High Plains with his brood mares and Morgan stud about the right time too. Only he's way too short and balding to be Jethro Markham.

Missing the tattoo as well. Stump just explained how we don't have no whores here in Lyons, but if we did, and a dirty old man got into town now and again, we'd soon know it if he had the Stars and Bars tattooed on his hide anywheres."

Stump said, "The Whipple place was deserted until recent, and it's easy to see how one dirty old man could be mistook for another. But Thorp Ralston's all right. We'd know if he was holding classes down there. From time to time he hires boys from town to chore for him. So it's as if we had our own spy corps keeping an eye on him. His only sin, so far, might be trespassing, should anyone ever run a title search on that property. The Whipples just died, natural, in that cruel winter we had under the Grant Administration. Ralston treats his day help fair and pays his bills in town on time. So we've had no call to pester him."

Longarm put his beer schooner down, with just a little left in it, as he said, soberly, "I'd like to have my own talk with your new nester. He doesn't describe to me like Jethro Markham either. But your point's well taken, and anyone can see how a would-be pupil of a famous crook could confuse one old gent in a remote riverside cabin with another."

Walt said, "Well, you only have to ride down the river past the first three cattle guards you'll see. Then you'll spy a stone chimney, standing alone in a grove of more recent aspen, and then you'll come to the old Whipple place, which is where Thorp Ralston's settled now. But I can tell you now what he'll tell you after you go to all that fool trouble."

Longarm said, "No, you can't. I have a photograph to show him, which you never did when he told you about those two mysterious saddle tramps."

The two local lawmen exchanged glances. Stump said, "They were right about this one. He's good. You stay here and have another if you've a mind to. But I'm riding with this Denver boy to watch him in action."

Walt put his own schooner down, saying, "Well, shit, I reckon I'm as anxious to learn as anyone else around here. So let's *vamanos, muchachos*."

Longarm had them put his McClellan and Winchester on the slower but steadier paint. Stump and Walt got their own ponies and stock saddles from out back of the town lockup and joined him near the livery. A couple of town idlers offered to tag along, if they wanted to wait up a few moments so everyone could ride out after the sons of bitches, but Stump explained this wasn't a posse gathering after all and they lost interest.

Longarm let his hosts lead the way, but wasn't surprised when they wound up following the South Saint Vrain, the Longmont Post Road, and the railroad tracks, all at the same time. Things had to work like that in the bumpier parts of the Front Range. In some stretches there was barely room for the river, road, and tracks to get through all at once. But wherever a few acres spread wider between the roaring little white-water river and the elephant-gray granite walls of its valley, some desperately ambitious folk had carved a bitty cattle empire or even sillier farmstead. His fellow lawmen tersely described the faces and fortunes of each household head in passing, and Longarm had to agree none sounded at all like the notorious Professor Markham.

As they passed a tangle of close-set aspen saplings with a lonely stone column barely visible, well back from the road, Walt cheerfully explained, "Some trappers built there, way back when, afore Boulder County got incorporated. The old-timers say the Kimaho burnt 'em out. I wouldn't know. I've never seen a Kimaho, if there's any left."

On Longarm's far side, Stump growled, "There ain't. There never were no Kimaho Indians. They're a made-up wonder like the hoop snake or the side-hill snorter."

Longarm didn't feel any call to mention those Kimaho sisters he'd met up with that time. He might have loved 'em and left 'em but he wasn't an infernal kiss-and-tell.

It was interesting, though, to note the opinionated county deputy didn't know quite as much about Boulder County as he let on.

Past the tanglewood, the second growth north of the riverside road had been cleared back a few hundred yards and fenced with three strands of Glidden Brand. An old weathered cabin with a new tar-paper roof stood halfway back to the far tree line, amid outbuildings with leaky-looking shingles. Another bobwire fence stretched across the belt-line of the modest spread and, sure enough, a dozen-odd scrub mares and a smug-looking Morgan stud were fenced in to graze that half of the cleared grassland.

As the three lawman negotiated the cattle guard between the front gateposts, a slender youth in bib overalls with no shirt came around one corner of an outbuilding, pitchfork in hand. When Walt waved, the kid waved back. Stump told Longarm, "That's be young Tim Cagney. Goes with Jim Hansen's daughter, and he'd best not knock her up if he knows what's good for him. He's a good kid, save for his horny nature. He must be helping old Thorp out here."

The squatter came out himself as the three of them reined in and dismounted in his dooryard. At first glance it was easy to see why Stump and Walt had dismissed him as the fugitive lifer, Markham. Longarm had caught up with enough wanted men to know an official description could be off more than a mite. But as they shook, in bright sunlight, he saw that Ralston's cheerful ruddy face was framed in thinning reddish hair instead of the thick salt and pepper mop that went with Markham. Ralston was about five foot eight, or average, in contrast to the six foot two or three they said Markham was. The clincher was the eye color. There was simply no way in hell a body could change his or her eye color, and Markham was said to have blue eyes, not hazel. So it would have been needlessly rude to ask the poor soul to take off his plaid shirt, and Longarm didn't.

As the kid with the pitchfork drifted in to join them, Stump explained what they were doing down this way.

Thorp Ralston nodded soberly and said, "You saved Tim, here, a drop-by on his way home. Tell 'em about that curious cuss who passed through this very damned day, Tim."

The younger hired hand shrugged awkwardly and asked, "What am I supposed to say, Mister Ralston? I never seen the cuss afore and you did most of the jawing with him."

Turning back to the lawmen, Ralston said, "That's true, to the extent he made any sense at all. He drifted in around nine or ten, wouldn't you say, Tim?"

The Cagney boy nodded and said, "Make her nine-thirty and I'll swear to her in court. From his jaded pony and damp duds I'd say he'd rid through the night and considerable rain before he got this far."

Ralston explained, "His mount was a roan with a lopsided white blaze as left its eyes mismatched. He said it was a good old mare when I asked. But you'd never sell me no pony with one eye brown and the other pink."

Longarm got out the sepia-tone as he replied in a firmly friendly voice, "I doubt there could be an arrest warrant out on his odd-looking mount. Before you tell me what he looked like, have a gander at the faces in this photograph. Might save us all some time."

But it didn't. Old Ralston vowed, and the kid agreed, that the rider they'd just mentioned had been someone else, although young Cagney requested a second look and decided, uncertainly, that he might have seen the one in the more sensible hat in town a time or two.

Longarm told them, "The one in the funny hat's a top hand called Lucky Lem. Since both an old sweetheart and a new employer feel he's missing, and since another cuss entire just turned up in Lucky Lem's fancy chaps, looking for trouble, I'd say there's a chance he's missing for good. The other young jasper was Rafe Farnsworth of the Rocking F near Trapper's Rock, the last time he was using his right name. If you both agree that wasn't him riding through here this morning, what say you describe that one after all?"

They did, to the disgust of all three experienced lawmen. For while both the old squatter and his mayhaps sharpereyed hand agreed on what the son of a bitch had looked like, there was little to inspire anyone in their description of an average-looking cuss in regular cowhand duds wearing his hat Colorado-style and his S&W sixgun, likely a .44, in a plain black leather side-draw gun rig.

When Longarm asked about hair and eye coloring, neither could say for certain. His rain-soaked broad-brimmed hat, dark gray or black, depending on how it dried out, had hidden his hair and shaded his eyes as he'd talked mostly to old Ralston in bright morning sunlight. So Longarm asked Ralston to repeat their conversation and the squatter explained, "That was the most interesting thing about the young cuss. It was like them earlier strangers I already reported to the law. He seemed to think there was something going on here that I must have missed as I was fixing the old place up. He said he had a couple of hundred dollars to give me, and asked if I'd trust him for the other fifty till he could put my teachings to good use. I told him I could teach him most anything I knew for way less than two hundred dollars, and then he started to ask really suspicious questions about men I'd never heard of and, oh, yeah, something about Idaho."

"It was Iowa," young Cagney chimed in, adding, "I remember because we come through Iowa on our way West when I was little. A lady in a nice-smelling apron come over to our camp after dark with a pie she'd baked and I mind my Daddy saying folk from Iowa was like that. That saddle tramp didn't look friendly, though, no matter where he's from."

Old Ralston nodded soberly and said, "Tim's right. It must have been Iowa he mentioned. Only he asked if I was from them parts. He never said *he* was. When I said I was Kentucky by birth and Colorado by choice, he stared at me sort of thundergasted, allowed he'd been given mighty dumb directions, and rid on in some haste."

Stump frowned thoughtfully and muttered; "I wonder where. I don't see how he could have ridden into Lyons aboard such an odd-looking mount, in broad-ass daylight, without at least one nosey Parker mentioning it to us."

Walt nodded and said, "We've been up and about since way afore nine-thirty, and we've asked the boys to keep us up to date on strangers riding in."

"You missed me," Longarm pointed out.

Stump grumbled, "Not for long. Not for all day. So what say we ride on back to town and ask around for the mysterious son of a bitch!"

Thorp Ralston asked if they didn't have time for at least a cup of coffee with him and his hand. Longarm respectfully declined and the three lawmen got back up to ride back to town. As they rode out of earshot, Walt asked Longarm how he knew old Thorp Ralston brewed leftover grounds in a tomato can. Longarm chuckled and replied, "I turned his coffee down more sincere than that. The day's not getting any younger and Lord knows how much scouting I'll be stuck with down this way. Unless you boys would like to help, I mean."

Stump and Walt exchanged puzzled looks. Stump decided, "We'd like to help, if you'd be kind enough to tell us what in the fuck we're supposed to be helping you with!"

Longarm pointed up the post road with his cheroot, saying, "I thought I'd start with that tanglewood where the Kimaho neglected to tear down that old chimney."

Stump started to ask why. But he'd hunted men on the dodge and likely desperate before. So he nodded and agreed. "Makes sense. Quaking aspen growing tight as ticks offers plenty of cover, whilst a fireplace still intact beats any other place in a tanglewood for a fire, and they did say the cuss looked as if he could use a good drying."

Walt, on the other side of the road, said, "Oh, sure, I get it. Even if he didn't hole up in them woods just ahead, it'll only take us a few minutes to bust through to the far side and make certain, right?"

Longarm let Stump reply. "Wrong. One of us lies low with his saddle gun on the far side whilst the other two flush him, riding through the saplings like a tribe of yapping Kimaho. If he's a stranger to these parts he might not know there ain't no Kimaho. Who gets to make the actual arrest, Longarm, you?"

The federal agent smiled wolfishly and replied, "I was afraid we were fixing to have a discussion about jurisdiction, pard. I'm glad you see Professor Jethro Markham's wanted federal until he does something serious in your county."

Stump grunted, "What jurisdiction? I just don't want to get killed, you ambitious asshole!"

Chapter 11

Longarm might have had a time pronouncing the fancy French term for it, but it still felt as if he'd been there before as he lay flat in damp pine needles with his Winchester trained south along the almost-solid wall of gray-green aspen trunks to his left. He'd chosen this corner of the overgrown quarter section because there didn't seem a better vantage point on this side, not because it seemed all that grand. Anyone busting out could just as easily bust out way the hell downslope, at long range in such tricky light. But having a cuss bust out *behind* you as you were covering the road at pistol range could leave you feeling even dumber, in such time as you might have left to feel anything.

As he lay there in the shimmering light, listening to unseen critters creaking in the forest duff while, way off in the distance, somebody seemed to be knocking a tree over, it came to Longarm where he'd felt like this before, staked out alone in a patch of greenwood with a clear field of fire ahead of him and Lord only knew how many sons of bitches creeping in behind him. He'd tethered his paint a furlong away amid the more open tree cover to the west. So there was nobody else within earshot as he softly murmured, "Shiloh!" and then shut up. He hadn't lived through that awful time in the wooded hills of Tennessee State by telling the whole damned world where they'd posted him with his own muzzle-loader and a young boy's heart beating fit to bust.

He was older now, and his Winchester could throw more rounds in a minute than he'd managed to get off in that whole first firefight.

Yet as ever, the grand notion he'd had, picking this particular spot to lie doggo, kept feeling dumber and dumber as he considered all the things that could go wrong.

It was tempting, now, to move closer to the river. For if that stranger to these parts was sort of feeling his way deeper into the mountains after getting the wrong directions, wouldn't he be likely to just go with the grain, closer to the river?

"Stay put," Longarm warned himself, even as he caught himself tensing to rise. For that first man he'd killed, way back when they'd both been no more than boys, had been the one who'd broken cover first, and there'd been many a time since when he'd survived by waiting out the other poor bastard just that vital minute longer.

Stump and Walt were working closer now, he could tell. They were good old boys who knew how to flush game the smart way, making just enough noise to let others hear they were coming without letting on they were anxious to flush anything or anybody. Longarm found it tough to locate them too exactly by their occasional thrashings and crashings. But he could tell they were getting closer, and he wasn't even worried about them spotting him. So if there was anybody worth flushing in that tanglewood . . .

And then there he was, big as life all at once, as if he'd been there all the time, as the shimmering dappled sunlight shifted just right. The man on foot led his head-down pony out of the aspen with the reins in his left hand as they followed the muzzle of his drawn sixgun in his right. Longarm made the range around twenty yards, and so far the simp hadn't even glanced his way. So he had the drop, but that drawn pistol gave him pause. He didn't want to kill any more of Professor Markham's pupils. Yet the proddy-looking young cuss was almost certain to whirl and fire without thinking if anyone called anything out to him.

And so, knowing this was a tad showboat and that nobody was ever going to speak to him again if he fucked up, Longarm fired and, wonder of wonders, blew that sixgun out of the other rider's hand, along with a good gob of the hand, without having to kill him.

Anyone else who was listening would have thought the noisy bastard had been killed, though, to hear him agonizing about it as he rolled on the ground, clutching his shattered right paw to his breast with the good left hand while his wall-eyed roan tore off through the trees and Longarm rolled to his own feet, calling out, "Aw, shut up, you ain't hurt that bad, pilgrim."

"That's a fucking lie and it hurts like hot brimstone, all the way up my arm!" wailed the wounded whatever as Longarm bore down on him, levering another round into the chamber of his Winchester. Off in the aspen Stump called out, "Did you get him, Longarm?"

To which Longarm cheerfully called back, "Yep, and better yet, in condition to talk!"

Then he kicked the cuss lying all curled up at his feet and told him to sit up and start talking. The kid with the shattered gun hand sobbed, "I got nothing to say to you, you cruel-hearted bushwhacker! What have I ever done to you to deserve such cruel and unusual punishment?"

Longarm cradled his carbine in the fork of a nearby tree and drew his own pistol as he hunkered down over his prey, saying, "That's one of the things we'll be talking about. I'm the law. You ain't. You just now asked directions to that institute of lower learning run by Jethro Markham and—"

"Who's Jethro Markham?" the shabby and now really muddy kid cut in, only to get himself cussed considerable and almost pistol-whipped, or so it seemed. For Longarm was hardly ever as evil-tempered as he liked crooks to think he might be.

Farther downslope Stump busted out of the aspen, pony and all. As he caught sight of the two others on the ground, Stump called, "Oh, there you are. What have we got there, pard?"

Longarm growled, "A total asshole, pretending to be even dumber. Stops at one spread asking for the way to Markham. Holes up right next door, and tries to tell us he don't know what we're talking about. Why don't you ride back and get Ralston and Cagney, Stump? It should only take a few minutes to prove that this is the jasper they turned in to us."

Stump knew how the game went. He replied, "Why don't we just gun him and say he tried to escape? That'd save everyone a heap of bother."

Longarm began to pat the wounded man down with his free hand as he replied, in a cold, uncaring tone, "Might not be such a bad idea. Anyone can see what a doctor bill someone's going to have to pay if this hand's to be saved. I wouldn't want to save the taxpayers the expense in front of taxpayers either, and we already know as much as this pissant could tell us if he wanted to."

The young stranger clutching that shattered hand to his bloody shirtfront sobbed, "Hold on now. You don't know all that much, for how much have I told you so far, you cruel cuss?"

Longarm pulled out the kid's wallet, flipped it open, and reading off the library card he found in it, said, "Well, Dwight Harcourt from Sharon Springs, Kansas, to begin with, we know you were directed to ride up the South Saint Vrain to the abandoned Whipple cabin and wait there with your money till a sort of school monitor came to lead you the rest of the way."

As Stump dismounted and Walt broke into view, Longarm called out, "He's got close to three hundred in silver certificates in this wallet. Would one of you go after his damned roan? We might be able to pin horse theft on him as well."

Walt whooped and rode on. Turning back to their prisoner, Longarm told him, pleasantly enough, "They still hang horse thieves in the state of Colorado, even when they steal those horses in west Kansas."

Harcourt whimpered, "I never stole old Pinkeye. He was given to me for my birthday, three years ago this fall."

Longarm put the wallet in one of his own side pockets, observing, "Your library card, dated last year, had you a high school senior when it was issued to you. Ain't you a little young to die, you dangerous criminal?"

Harcourt whined, "I don't want to die, Mister Longarm. Can't you let me off with just this dreadful injury? I've never done anything really wrong to anybody. I swear to God I ain't the outlaw you seem to take me for!"

Longarm told him, "Don't you really mean not yet? We know all about Professor Markham and the swell pointers he gives on stopping trains and robbing stages for fun and profit. I reckon when you run off to be a big bad desperado when you grew up, it never occurred to you that you might not grow up, or that it hurt so much to get hit by a bullet, eh?"

Harcourt was crying real tears now as he replied, "I figured it hurt. I never knew it felt awful as *this* and I no-shit need me a doctor, bad!"

Longarm snorted in derision and said, "Shit, wait till you wind up gutshot, or even hit somewhere less fatal, like through the spine. I only winged you gentle, just now. But would you really like us to take you into town alive and see if the doc could save that hand?"

Harcourt said he would, and that he'd do anything, any damn thing at all, if only they'd have mercy on him. So Longarm helped the hurt boy to his feet, growling, "Well, I've never liked boys all that much. So I'll have to settle

145

for you singing the whole song to us, as good as you know how."

Then they wrapped his gun-shot hand in a damp kerchief and had him singing like a canary all the way back to town.

So they'd taken down Dwight Harcourt's sworn statement and gotten him to sign it, left-handed, before supper time. By then the elderly sawbones who got to bill the law for such services had tidied up the shattered hand, encased it in a plaster cast, and opined that the young rascal would never make much of a gunslick now, whether infection set in or not. Longarm still insisted, and the sheriff's department agreed, some back-checking was in order before they let anyone calling himself Dwight Harcourt loose, although the tale he told of his criminal career, so far, read more silly than serious.

Harcourt allowed he'd been brought up by kind parents on a west Kansas homestead, where they'd raised grass-hoppers, hogs, and dent corn in about that order. A neighbor youth he'd smoked corn silk with when they'd been younger had told him about the swell lessons Professor Markham was offering in the wilder cattle country of Colorado for just a hundred and fifty dollars. Harcourt identified the one who'd led him astray as one Larry White. From the description, White sounded a heap like one of those boys killed under another name down Denver way, and when Longarm flashed a photograph of the body some joker had shipped home to Boulder as the late Rafe Farnsworth, Harcourt blanched, allowed that was his old pal, Larry White, and asked what might have happened to him.

Longarm told him there was no might about it. So now they knew how little names meant to wayward youths Pro-fessor Markham had had time to instruct on such matters. There was an outside chance Dwight Harcourt hadn't stolen his present name and I.D. yet. So Longarm went over to the Western Union to see about that.

First things coming first, he untethered his hired pony

out front to ride it the short hop to the livery, where he asked them to rub it down good and ration it the extra oats he felt it deserved.

Then he strode over to the Peakview Hotel to hire himself a room for the night no matter how the night turned out. He'd never figured how they knew, but he did know that women just never invited a man in out of the rain when he had no place else on earth to go in the wee small hours.

Then, having assured his basic comforts, if not any luxuries in particular, he went on to the Western Union where, sure enough, he found that strawberry blonde with the bun full of pencils still on duty. She looked as happy to see him and asked if that other lawman had caught up with him. When he asked what other lawman they could be jawing about, she said, "His name was Gilroy, I do believe. Said he was from other parts and that he had important news to share with you."

Longarm ran the name through his memory, shrugged, and said, "I can't say I know him. Might he have said he was from other parts like Iowa or even Kansas?"

She said she didn't recall the mysterious lawman offering any mailing address. Longarm said, "Well, if he comes by again you might tell him I'm staying at the Peakview. Now I need the telegraph address of the Kansas sheriff's department that goes with Sharon Springs, to begin with."

By the time she'd looked it up and established they were talking about Wallace County, Longarm had about blocked out his request for any yellow sheets they might have on their Dwight Harcourt, along with some means of identifying the wayward young cuss for certain.

As she read it over before sending it she said, "Good heavens, you have had a busy day, haven't you?"

He smiled thinly and warned her, "We're not half started. I forgot a name, so let me see that form again."

She did and he asked Wallace County what, if anything, they might have on another local boy called Larry White. Then he confided, "You're right about it having been a busy

147

day. I'm starting to think sleepy-headed and I ain't even had my supper yet."

She asked him, archly, what sort of thoughts he had the most trouble with when he was fixing to go to bed. He laughed and said, "Lord willing and the creeks don't rise, I might just get to bed by midnight at the rate I'm going. I got oodles of other wires to send once you're done sending that one."

So she said, "Oh," in a small sad voice, and went back to put his first message on the wire as he busied himself writing others. He was faster with a pencil than she was with a telegraph key, and she had to piddle with other fists wanting to use the same lines. So by the time she rejoined him he was about done, for now. But she stared down at his sheaf of filled-out forms in dismay, saying, "Good grief! Those are sure to take me the better part of an hour and it's almost quitting time!"

He glanced at the wall clock, saw she was full of it, and said soothingly, "This is nothing to the final report I hope to wire when and if I ever put this puzzle together right. I keep thinking I got a handle on it, but every time I get a piece to fit I'll be switched if another piece don't pop out of nowheres at me."

She didn't look any happier. So he added, "Tell you what I'm going to do. Once you finish up here I'm going to take you across the way for some supper or at least some coffee and cake, and then if you'd like, I'll walk you home and we'll see what happens after that."

She heaved a great sigh and replied, "I'd love to see what happens after that, but I room with other young ladies under the watchful eye of a landlady who rides brooms on Halloween, some say. Even if I didn't, a girl has to watch her reputation in a town this size, and roaming in the gloaming with handsome strangers isn't the way one establishes her undoubted virginity."

Longarm nodded soberly and asked, "How about that coffee and cake anyways, no strings?"

To which she demurely replied, "Maybe. Why don't you come back around six and we'll see."

He hadn't planned on leaving. On the other hand he was starting to get hungry again and there'd be nothing to do here, with her in the back going clickety-clack. So he nodded, said he'd make sure the coffee shop across the way was clean and decent, and turned to leave.

Then the county lawman Walt came through the front door the other way, blinked at Longarm in mild surprise, and asked, "How'd you find out already?"

Longarm asked what he'd just found out and Walt said, "Rider just come down from Association Camp. Should have reported it to Larimer County but what do hard-rock miners know."

"Not much about jurisdiction," Longarm agreed. "What did your hard-riding hardrocker have to report?"

Walt said, "Attempted train robbery. Some old boys with feed sacks over their fool heads tried to pull a Jesse James on the narrow-gauge where it runs along the Big Thompson. The train crew figures they might have winged one or more in the resulting running gunfight. Stump just told me to put out an all-points no matter whose county the no-goods rid to!"

Longarm said that made sense and added, "I'm going across the way for a bite to eat. If you need me and I ain't there, I'll most likely be at the Peakview."

He started to move on, snapped his fingers, and turned back to Walt to say, "There I go again. Has another lawman from out of town been asking for me over to your lockup, Walt?"

When Walt said no Longarm frowned. "Thin air up this way might be getting to him too. He said his name was Gilroy. The blonde lady here can describe him way better than me if he winds up missing as well. I'll check with you later, Walt."

The local lawman didn't seem to care. Longarm went across to the place he'd already picked out and decided, once he was seated at the marble counter, it was good enough for him but a tad unromantic to invite a lady on your first walk-home with her. The gal behind the counter was pleasantly plump too. He suspected the one who worked across the street might lunch here regular. He didn't ask. Women always found out you'd asked about 'em, even in way bigger towns than this, and it seemed to give them the notion you really wanted 'em.

He told the plump henna-headed waitress he wanted chili over that fancy omelet they said was special on that blackboard. When he told her he'd have both the chocolate custard and peach cobbler listed as desserts, she blinked owlishly at him and explained, "You don't get two desserts with one entree, cowboy."

To which he replied, not unkindly but firmly, "Sure I do. Didn't you just hear me order both? I've had a long day. I might have a long night. I've found I stay awake better with both some sweets and coffee in me and I still prefers my coffee black, so . . . "

"You have to pay extra here for anything extra," she said.

Longarm nodded and said, "*Bueno*. Mix an order of the Spanish rice I see on your blackboard with my omelet and chili con carne, as long as I'm dining on the cart, as they say in Paris and Saint Louis these days. That ought to hold me till bedtime, if I don't stay up too late."

She told him it ought to make him sick too. But he agreed that as long as he was paying à la carte he could eat most anything they had on hand.

Then she watched in envy as he put it all away. When it came time for him to pay up, she confided she had a sweet tooth on top of her craving for bread and, damn it, look how fat she was even after all that self-denial!

As she gave him back his change and they somehow wound up holding hands, Longarm told her, "It ain't so much what you eat as how you burn it up inside. I ain't a cowboy. I got a job that sometimes works me even harder. I can see you're on your feet all day here. But if you really want to get away with sweets on top of solid food, you ought to stay up later, after work."

She protested, "There's nothing to do here in Lyons, after dark, most nights. I do kick up my heels every time there's a dance at the grange hall but . . . Come to study on it, I do turn in early, alone with a box of chocolates and a sad book, most every night."

He let her keep the change so he could get his hand back and quit while he was ahead. It would have been cruel to tell a lonesome fat gal how to get more exercise after dark unless he was willing to sort of work out with her, and the blonde across the way was prettier as well as a tad less stout.

But when he got back to Western Union he found a prune-faced old fart with a bald dome and green eyeshade behind the counter. He asked how come and the night man said, "If you're asking about Billie Peters, she just left. If you're the cuss she said she'd wait a few more minutes for, I can see why she flounced out so pissed. Don't you know how hard it can be to meet young single gals in a town this size, cowboy?"

Longarm said he was neither a cowboy nor planning on staying all that long. He introduced himself. They jawed for a time about that half-ass attempt on the narrow-gauge up along the Big Thompson, and when Longarm asked if there was anything new on that, the night man shook his eyeshade and replied, "Not if you were here when that rider came in from the hard-rock country on a mighty lathered pony. Everyone's supposed to watch out for a gang of four, if they ain't split up by now. Damn fools tried to stop a moving train by just riding alongside, waving guns at the engineer. At least one of the masked men was hit mighty serious and couldn't have rid far. Another, in a red and black checkerboard shirt, lost his hat and swayed in the saddle considerable after the brakeman let fly. They figure he could be wounded slight or serious, and wasn't he an asshole to act so wild in such a wild shirt?"

Longarm nodded and muttered, "Green kids who've read

too many Ned Buntline tales of the opportunities for advancement out our way, most likely. I wish old Ned would quit writing that shit. It makes my job sort of tedious, at times."

He got out two cheroots, handed one to the ugly but otherwise pleasant night man, and lit them both before he headed up the walk toward his hotel in the orange and lavender light of a mountain gloaming. He'd been stating the pure truth when he'd said the thinner air up this way made for sharper appetites and duller thoughts. He thought swell down in Denver, even if it as a mile above sea level. Lyons wasn't really that much higher. It was possible he was as confused by all the razzle-dazzle as anything else. That damned old Jethro Markham had his pupils listed under all sorts of confusing names, twisted out of real names to make it even more confusing, and as if that wasn't enough, some of the infernal suspects couldn't be made to fit into any sensible pattern under any damned names at all!

It seemed obvious that mysterious moron wearing Lucky Lem's fancy hat and chaps had done something wicked to Lucky Lem. Only where might that mesh with Kitty's kid brother, Rafe Farnsworth, or with Lucky Lem?

That Harcourt boy from Kansas had just now sworn he'd never heard of either young Farnsworth or Lucky Lem. He hadn't been much help with the trainees Markham had sent down to intercept the Larkin brothers with that loot from the Indian Nation either. Unaware how ferociously his teeth were bared around his cheroot, Longarm growled, "Nothing a single crook has pulled off so far makes a lick of sense for a crook of average experience, let alone a master criminal, unless I'm missing something important. So what's so blamed important that I'm still missing, damn it?"

Nobody out on the street seemed likely to tell him as the sun sank ever lower and those not already having supper seemed to be headed for some. As he approached the front entrance of his hotel Longarm shot a disgusted look up at the sky and muttered, "Shit, you're fixing to just toss and turn like an earthworm on a slate walk if you call it a day this early with nothing on your mind but the dumb doings of assholes who won't even give their right names!"

There was a dinky tobacco shop catty-corner across the way. So Longarm headed there instead of turning right in at the Peakview. He purchased a fresh supply of three-for-a-nickel cheroots, the latest *Police Gazette,* a day-late *Denver Post,* and next month's edition of *Scientific American.* As he paid the old tobacconist off he explained with a sheepish smile, "I can't understand a lot of the stuff they print in *Scientific American,* but that helps me get sleepy, and sometimes I even learn something."

The old-timer said he wouldn't know, since he only sold 'em. Longarm put the fresh smokes away, rolled up the newspaper and magazines, and headed back to the Peakview. As he was crossing the street he saw, from this angle, there was a side entrance facing him, a tad closer, and he was bad as a cat about exploring any new surroundings he might find himself in. So he swerved to enter the hotel lobby via that route without having to think about it twice.

The lobby hadn't changed, but did look somewhat different as one came in via the side door. He hadn't noticed a cuspidor here and a paper palm tree there, signing in before. The same clerk looked a tad different as he stood behind the same desk, talking to a younger gent dressed cow, with his gun worn side-draw and his hat crushed Colorado. Neither noticed Longarm coming toward them. He had plenty of time to study the two of them. It didn't take him all that long to whip out his .44–40 and snap, "Grab for the ceiling, Roberts!"

The gunslick Longarm was training a gun on shot both empty hands up like sky rockets, going frog-belly pale and clammy as he screamed like a schoolmarm who'd just had a mouse run under her skirts. As Longarm moved in to place his reading material on the counter and disarm the frightened rascal, his victim pissed in his pants and sobbed, "Don't do me like you done old Bobby, Longarm! I swear we never meant you no harm!"

The room clerk stared thundergasted at both of them to declare, as if he knew, "That's right, Deputy Long! Ranger Gilroy here just came by for a friendly visit. I was just now telling him you were out and—"

"He said he'd wait," Longarm cut in, smiling thinly at the man he had the drop on as he continued. "This sneak ain't no lawman and his real name's Roberts. You just heard him say we got his twin brother, Bobby, over to the undertaker's. That'd make this . . . who?"

The more sensibly dressed but otherwise identical twin of the one Longarm had shot it out with in front of that chili joint gulped hard and said, "I'm Freddy Roberts, the innocent one. It was Bobby you wanted all the time, Longarm. I was just tagging along. I swear I've never done wrong in all my born days."

Longarm placed the punk's pistol on the counter and said, "Now turn and plant both palms on that marble whilst I pat you down for French postcards and such. We'll talk about your innocent past at the lockup down the street, Roberts. There's another desperado there I'd like you to meet."

Chapter 12

An older florid-faced lawman was seated at the main desk when Longarm frog-marched Freddy Roberts in at gunpoint. But the deputy called Stump had just come back from supper, figuring it might be one of those nights, so he was able to vouch for all present who might need it as he introduced Longarm and Undersheriff Baker, in command of the Lyons office.

As they shook, Baker glanced at the hangdog Freddy Roberts and asked what they might have here. Longarm nodded at Stump, who nodded back and said, "He's got to be kin to that one Longarm shot earlier, Boss. Stretch 'em nekked on slabs in the same morgue and you'd have a hell of a time telling one from the other."

"I want a lawyer!" wailed Freddy Roberts as they all looked him up and down with clinical detachment.

Undersheriff Baker told him, "You'll get a lawyer after we book you and not before. What kind of a sissy jail do you think I'm running here?" Then he turned to Longarm to ask, "What might we be booking him for, attempted murder?"

Longarm shook his head and replied, "It was his brother who attempted flat out in front of witnesses. I got the drop on this one with only a hotel clerk to back me, and all I can prove in court is that he told a few fibs. I can't say I heard him. He didn't have the balls to lie to me either. So if his lawyer shoots for one man's word against another, and he surely ought to, if he knows his trade—"

"Aw, shit," Baker cut in. "What did you bring him here for if you don't have anything to charge him with?"

Longarm said, "I never told you that. I only said I didn't have anything personal against the shit-for-brains. I call him that because I suspect he was laying for me just now with a view to paying me back for his brother and, ah, personal reasons I don't want to drag any innocent lady's name through."

"He's crazy, Sheriff!" Roberts protested, with a little more blood coming back to his rat face, now that he saw nobody seemed likely to just gun him out of hand.

Undersheriff Baker smiled mildly up at Longarm to ask, "*Are* you crazy? I don't like the looks of this one, and his dead brother was a shit for certain, but what's he *done* if you don't want him arrested?"

Longarm replied, "I never said he shouldn't be arrested. I just said it had little or nothing to do with me. Lucky Lem Corrigan, the true owner of a mighty big hat and some mighty fancy chaps, was a top hand this shit and his twin brother envied, a good day's ride to the south but still within your county jurisdiction if you'd like credit for solving the murder in an election year."

Baker said he'd like that a heap but added, "Who'd they murder, this top hand they had it in for?"

Longarm nodded and replied, soberly, "Lucky Lem was no doubt easy to feel jealous around. He was flashy, popular, and in sum, everything this trash-white and his no-good twin were not. They were best known down near the county seat for cruelty to animals and vicious practical jokes. That's not a good way to attract any young gals a man might want

156

to wind up with. Lucky Lem was way better at that. So he had a serious understanding with at least one local belle neither twin could even get a tender glance from."

Turning back to Freddy Roberts, Longarm favored him with a disgusted smile and declared, "You should have just let Corrigan ride on up here and take that job with the Lazy Four, Freddy. He was likely as stuck on himself as you and your twin suspected. He'd have likely found a new sweetheart up this way. I noticed, riding up here from Boulder, what a ride that would be just to get laid."

Freddy Roberts said Longarm was just talking dirty and that neither he nor his poor dead brother had been out to lay anybody.

Longarm said, "Let's not go into anyone up here or down Boulder way you might have had hot jeans for, Freddy. You and Bobby laid for Lucky Lem along that same trail, and we all know why he never got here. It was dumb as hell to keep that dead man's fancy outfit, no matter how much you admired it. I guess you told Bobby that, though, right?"

Roberts said, "I want a lawyer. Nobody's putting no words in my mouth without I see a lawyer first."

Undersheriff Baker beamed and said, "My, don't he talk educated about such matters, though? You reckon he's been taking lessons from that Professor Markham?"

Longarm said, "I doubt it. If he has, he ought to demand his money back. The way I put it together, this moron and his twin ganged up on the Corrigan boy I just mentioned with little more thought and no more motive than a pair of cur dogs fighting over a bitch in heat. That's the only way subhuman shits like them regard romance. It didn't do them a lick of good to murder Lucky Lem, of course, save for the way old Bobby wound up with his hat and chaps. The high-born lady all the fuss was over barely knew they were alive, even after they'd killed her sweetheart. Let's not go into how they might have decided she liked me too. Suffice it to say they must have. So they decided to go after me next, in their own yellow-dog style. I spied them dogging

157

me at a mighty safe distance, waiting for a chance to jump me two to one as I lay fast asleep. I threw them off. But they knew I'd wind up here in Lyons sooner or later, so they got here sooner. They never planned on my bumping noses with just one of them, like I did out front of that chili joint. But when I did, Bobby lost his head. So this poor shit tried for me tonight, hoping to ambush me as I returned to the Peakview. He didn't have the balls to fight man to man."

"You had the drop on me," Freddy Roberts protested. Then he said, "I don't know why my brother wanted to fight you. I only wanted to ask you about that this evening, damn it."

Longarm chuckled and told Baker, "You're right, he's been taking lessons, if only in some pool hall. He still thinks he can wriggle out of it."

Baker asked, "Can he wriggle out of it? It ain't that you don't make a heap of sense, Longarm, but we do need us one of them delicate corpses if we mean to hang this rascal."

Longarm nodded and said, "The only question before the house is whether they killed Lucky Lem alone or another missing boy as well. I know they killed somebody, because once you've been through a war you never mistake the reek of a dead human from the stink of, say, a dead cow."

He saw that had drained some blood from Freddy Roberts's cheeks indeed. So choosing his words carefully, Longarm softly said, "You shouldn't have spooked me like that, up in the hills, Freddy. Had I ridden up here the shorter and more sudden way, I might never have drifted by that wild and lonely spot you left poor Lucky Lem to rot."

The accused killer gasped, "That's a lie. You're just making that up! You never rid nowhere's near the hollow we buried him and . . . " Then he gave a strangled cry and keeled over in a dead faint as he saw what he'd just given away, in front of more than one witness.

Baker growled, "We'd best have the doc look him over after we lock him up in the back. Getting a full confession from a jasper subject to fainting spells is going to be a bitch."

Longarm said, "You'll get one, given smelling salts and some time for him to get used to the notion. I'd like to stick Boulder County with all the paperwork, if it's at all possible."

Baker chuckled fondly and said, "I don't see what's impossible about Boulder County trying one of its own for killing one of its own in an election year."

Longarm said, "I was hoping you'd feel that way. The only loose end I'd like to tie up involves any connection this unconscious asshole and his twin brother might have had with Professor Jethro Markham."

So Baker had his deputies haul Roberts back to the cell block and ask young Harcourt if he'd ever seen this other asshole before.

When the wounded would-be pupil of the criminal college avowed he had not, and politely asked what this was all about, Longarm was the one who told him, "Forget it. We've wired your hometown and if it turns out you're the nitwit you say you are, you might just get out of this with your neck the same length. I hate to admit it, but you've got a swell alibi for that attempted train robbery this afternoon."

Harcourt asked what train robbery. The lawmen exchanged glances and Baker said, "You just hug your busted hand and ponder some more on the error of your ways, Harcourt. You other boys, roll Roberts in cell three and empty a pail over him."

Longarm murmured, "Thought you were going to have the doc look at him. You wouldn't want him dying of a heart-stroke on you before you can teach him the rope dance, do you?"

Baker thought, shrugged, and said, "Forget the bucket and fetch the doc, Jim." Then he turned back to Longarm to announce, "I'd say this calls for a drink, and it so happens I got a bottle of bourbon filed under B, out front."

Longarm agreed that sounded mighty efficient, and followed Baker and Stump back out front while the lockup crew tidied up in the back.

But that bourbon was not to be after all. For they'd no sooner made it to the vicinity of that filing cabinet when the door burst open and Walt came in, out of breath, to announce, "Shootout, down at the old Whipple place!"

Baker said, "You mean the spread Thorp Ralston's resettled? Who shot whom, over what?"

Walt said, "Thorp Ralston just rid in, hit in the thigh. He's over at the doc's right now. He tells us he left his hired hand, the Cagney boy, dead or dying in the company of a total stranger he just had to kill. Doc says Ralston ain't hurt bad, but he's surely shook up."

Undersheriff Baker slammed the filing cabinet shut again, saying, "If he can talk at all I'd surely like a word with him!"

Longarm snubbed out his cheroot, dropped the butt in a spittoon by the desk, and muttered, "Me too. But you boys go along and I'll join you at the doc's once I fetch me a pony from the livery."

Baker blinked, started to say something dumb, and replied, "Oh, right, we'll all want to ride on to Ralston's cabin, no matter what he says just happened there!"

Longarm had no trouble finding the doc's place in the gathering dusk. For he'd asked directions at the livery while they were saddling Brandy for him. He tethered the cordovan mare out front, with the half-dozen county mounts already there, and the doc's plain but sweet-mannered wife let him in and led the way back to their clinic, where he found Baker and the other local lawmen gathered around the wounded Thorp Ralston and the same old G.P. who'd patched up Harcourt's hand at the lockup down the slope. As Longarm joined them, Undersheriff Baker waved the notebook in his hand and softly explained, "We was about to leave for Thorp's cabin. I got it all down, such as it is."

Longarm told them to just go along and he'd catch up, having a fast pony and knowing the way. Baker cocked a brow and replied, "Not hardly. It's a joy to watch you work, Longarm. So pester away and let's see if I missed anything."

It appeared in the end that Baker hadn't. The doc had given old Ralston something for the pain that made him stare up fuzzy and smile at the wrong things. But the tale he told as the doc went on cleaning the one plump naked thigh seemed simple enough.

The horse-breeding squatter said young Tim Cagney had planned on staying the night to get an early start in the morning. They'd just supped, and Tim was doing the dirty dishes on the back porch, when he heard something pestering the ponies pastured out back. Tim had lit a bull's-eye lantern and gone upslope for a look-see, packing no more than a pitchfork. Ralston allowed it was mighty lucky he'd trailed after with his trusty Henry, fearing it might be a lobo or even a bear that far up in the hills.

He giggled, glassy-eyed, and said, "It all happened faster than it takes to say it. All of a sudden there was this other young cuss in the beam of Tim's lantern. Then he shot Tim down like a dog, and even though I couldn't see him after that, I got lucky, firing at the after-image of his muzzle flash. For even though I got hit and knocked down almost the same time, I found out what a swell shot I'd been when I crawled over to Tim, made sure he was dead, and swept the beam of his fallen bull's-eye up the slope. I shot the cuss I saw there again, to make sure. Then I somehow made her back to the corral, climbed aboard old Midnight, and rid on into town, bareback without a bridle. Midnight sure earned his keep tonight!"

Baker murmured, "Midnight would be Thorp's Morgan stud. He keeps it penned close to the cabin at night for obvious reasons."

The owner of the famous horse croaked, "That's what they must have been after, fresh mounts. I wish Tim hadn't heard 'em and got kilt like so, the poor young cuss!"

Longarm asked, "They?" Seeing Ralston seemed out of it, he turned to Baker, who explained, "He said, before, he thought there was more than one. He heard someone riding off as he lay wounded, and there's no way the one he shot could have ridden off, right?"

Longarm agreed that made sense and suggested they go see. So they did. It didn't take long to ride down the South Saint Vrain to the scene of woe. But word had spread like wildfire, and so they arrived to find dozens of torch-waving neighbors endangering the property with careless flames and the evidence with their damned feet.

The flickering torchlight and shifting black shadows made for a mighty confused survey of the premises as the lawmen dismounted in the dooryard, tethered their ponies amid all the others they found there, and strode around to the back.

A pitchfork stood upright a dozen yards from the back door, its tines driven deep in the dirt. Undersheriff Baker asked where the hired hand who'd been packing it when he'd been hit might be. An even older gent with a nightshirt tucked into his jeans explained, "They carried Tim Cagney back to his poor old widowed mamma. Zeb Lovett druv the fork lying next to the body into the ground to mark the spot Tim died. We knew you boys would want to know."

Longarm started to ask a question. But Baker was too quick, and just as smart, it seemed. It was Baker who asked exactly where Tim Cagney had been hit, and with what.

Another neighbor volunteered. "Dead center in the breastbone. Neat blue hole about the right size for a .45. The mother-fucker who shot Tim is still yonder, against the bobwire, if you'd like to look him over. He ain't got no kin in these parts to claim him, far as we know."

With Baker leading the way they all strode north across the barnyard until, sure enough, the torchlight picked up a figure half seated and half sprawled against a fence post. One of the earlier arrivals said, "Back of his shirt's hung up on a barb."

Baker asked them to give him more light on the subject and hunkered down by the dead stranger, opening the front of the dark blue shirt and taking a thoughtful look before he grunted, "Hit twice, like Thorp said. Fair marksmanship too. Either round would have finished this skinny young shit."

His deputy called Walt said, "I've seen him around town a time or two. Never asked him who he might be, so he never told me."

Longarm asked for a torch and, once he got it, held it down closer to make certain before he nodded, handed the torch back, and told them, "His name was Raphael Farnsworth, no matter what he might have changed it to for outlaw reasons. His father's Major Farnsworth of the Rocking F, down by Trapper's Rock, and he has an older sister, Miss Judith, as well. If you'd like me to prove all this, I got this sepia-tone of him and the late Lucky Lem Corrigan, taken down Boulder way by the illegitimate child of Louis Daguerre."

Undersheriff Baker was neither as well-read nor possessed of a dry sense of humor. As he studied the photograph by torchlight he said, "Those sure are the chaps that Roberts twin was wearing when you shot it out with him, and anyone can see this other young jasper in the picture looks exactly like this dead cuss here. Only, who in thunder might Louis Daguerre be and where might he fit in?"

Longarm sighed and said, "I was only funning. Or mayhaps I was only observing how even otherwise honest men make up tall stories and new identities for themselves. Forget the photographer down Boulder way. Suffice it to say that after young Farnsworth here had his picture taken with a pal who was sparking his sister, he got to talking to someone more sinister and ran off to join Professor Markham, not long after they let the old crook out of Iowa State Prison.

163

We've already been over the sad story of Lucky Lem and the murderous twin you've got on ice, for it will doubtless fill in any gaps as you take down his full confession."

Walt asked, "What if he refuses to confess everything?" Baker told him to stop talking dumb and let Longarm have his full say.

So Longarm said, "You boys have about caught up with me for now. Being one of Markham's first pupils, this young smart-ass may well have been entrusted with some errands, practical jokes and such. I've got it fairly well established that new recruits were directed to some out-of-the-way place, when one or more gang members picked them up and walked 'em the rest of the way to school after making sure they hadn't been followed."

Walt opined, "That accounts for 'em shifting their operation up our way once them Cherokee Police trailed the Larkin boys to that soddy down your way, right?"

Undersheriff Baker nodded before Longarm could and said, "I'll bet anything Jethro Markham's mysterious crime college is still about where he established it after escaping from prison. Look about you and try her this way, boys. Say they started out using this old Whipple spread whilst it was still deserted. When Thorp Ralston and his breeding stock showed up to reclaim and fix up the old tumbledown cabin, they had the choice of gunning Ralston even earlier or using another out-of-the-way stopover. Markham recalled the homestead claim of his dead cell-mate, what's his name, and—"

"Paget, Hiram Paget," Longarm cut in. "It's my practice to memorize the serious names I put in my notebook. Saves looking 'em up when I'm pressed for time."

Baker grimaced and said, "Whatever. Markham would have figured the dead man's abandoned spread was a safe haven because only he knew Paget was dead. Only, thanks to you and them Cherokee Police, that cover was uncovered too, and so all we have to figure out is the professor's next port of call."

Walt smiled and said, "By jimmies, they might even be stuck with their one main hideout and no way station at all. They can't use that soddy down near Denver. They can't use this old cabin here, so—"

"Why did this dead cuss come here then?" Longarm asked. "By the way, I don't see any gun on the ground around here, and didn't Thorp say he heard hoofbeats *after* he gunned this cuss?"

Baker told Stump and Walt to fan out for sign. Then, addressing the crowd, he announced, "Look here, friends and fellow Republicans, the collection of souvenirs is one thing and the withholding of evidence is another. So who picked up this bastard's gun?"

Nobody answered. Baker glared, called them fucking Democrats, and turned back to Longarm, growling, "Well, it hardly seems likely he knocked Cagney and Ralston down with his fists. Try this on for size, Longarm. We only got a partial description of them failed train robbers up along the Big Thompson. But the timing and the known inclinations of this dead shit work out. At least two of his sidekicks were hit and may not have made it half this far. So say young Farnsworth here, and the one Ralston heard riding off, forgot this old hideout had been taken over by others, or just didn't give a damn about old Thorp, knowing he had fresh mounts for the taking here?"

Longarm pursed his lips, consulted his mental map of the Front Range, and allowed, "Well, we're talking twenty or thirty miles, with some high rough country between, and they'd have had to change mounts some damned where and sudden, no matter what their final destination."

Baker nodded and said, "I doubt the two wounded made her this far, and the gang never could have been all that big, even before it started to get whittled down so good of late. So how do you cotton to the notion that that last one, riding off from here this very night, was Jethro Markham in the flesh!"

Longarm said, "I'd love it. But it's ever best to ponder all the facts you know for certain before you start blowing pretty bubbles in the air. Don't you reckon we ought to cut that other rider's trail before we decide in advance who we're trailing?"

Baker demanded one of those damned torches and rolled through the bobwire with it as Longarm followed. The unsaddled remuda of brood mares that were supposed to be grazing on that side favored them with wary red-eyed glances and edged further upslope. Walt rode in from their left, opining, "If he headed back to town it wasn't aboard no horse, Boss. There's many a hoofprint on this side of old Thorp's fence, of course, but no place anyone led a mount through, even if you could do that without opening a gate."

Baker asked, "What about that Dwight Harcourt you brung in earlier, hand-shot? Didn't you catch him in the aspen to the west, pink-eyed pony and all?"

Walt laughed and said, "Hell, Boss, you must not have been listening. Young Harcourt left this property by way of the post road after asking directions in vain to Outlaw Tech."

Baker grimaced and said, "Right. Lucky for him he got here too late to take part in that half-ass attempt on that narrow-gauge. Longarm here refuses to believe the professor himself led the class in a sort of practical test."

Before Longarm could protest he was only trying to keep an open mind about a gang that couldn't even keep its own names straight, Stump came in from the east to report, "*Nada*. Don't see how anyone could have got through the fence without leaving a trace, and the back line of this claim runs along rock I'd hate to ride over on a bighorn. But what if both outlaws had their ponies on the other side of the wire all the time?"

Baker nodded gravely and said, "That works. Young Cagney said he heard something over this way. He never said just where because they gunned him before he could have. Say they tethered their own mounts most anywhere in the barnyard, moved over this way, searching for the gate in the dark, and—"

"Called out for that pretty gal locked in the tower to let down her hair," Longarm cut in, sounding mighty disgusted as he insisted, "You're blowing pretty bubbles again, Baker. All we know for certain is what Thorp Ralston told us, full of dope with the doc still working on him."

Baker growled, "All right. Seeing as you're so smart, where do you think we'll catch up with that other outlaw, no matter whether he's the mastermind or not?"

Longarm reached for a smoke, saying, "Not around here. That's all I do know for certain. With no trail to follow in this light, I for one intend to sleep on it and get a fresh start in the sane light of dawn."

Baker sighed and said, "You may be right. Hey, wait, where's the pony this dead one rid in on, if it wasn't him Thorp heard riding out?"

Longarm said, "I was wondering when you'd notice."

Chapter 13

Hardly anything was open in town when Longarm dismounted by the livery. So he got a good night's sleep alone. It didn't leave him with any permanent injuries, and he got an early start on the remaining outlaws and anyone else who wanted to make something of it when he ordered flapjacks with corn syrup and fried eggs over chili con carne at that same place across from the Western Union.

The same fat henna-haired gal was behind the counter when he did this. She asked dubiously if he was aware of what he'd just said, and when he explained he wanted the orders on separate chinaware, she still warned him he was asking for an early grave from indigestion.

He allowed he'd better have plenty of black coffee to rinse it down and mayhaps dilute it some. So she watched with awe as he put away enough to make some sissies sick, even if they hadn't sprinkled extra tabasco sauce over the chili and eggs.

She murmured, "My heavens, you must be a man of iron, and did I mention last night that they're fixing to have a barn-raising this weekend, with music and refreshments for one and all?"

Before he could answer, the local lawman called Walt came in, sat down beside Longarm, and said, "Just picked up a wire from Loveland Township on the Big Thompson. Two down and two to go. I've just time for coffee and mayhaps one sinker, Martha."

As the counter-gal served him, Longarm asked if Walt would like to elaborate just a tad. So his fellow lawman nodded and said, "Two bodies wearing feed-sack masks and devoid of any pocket money showed up in the shallows where the Big Thompson slows down for all them irrigation works near Loveland Township. Larimer County opines, and I agree, it looks as if the survivors dumped the wounded boys in white water to get rid of 'em and confuse us more. It ain't clear whether the dead ones died from their wounds or got some help in calling it the end when they couldn't go on."

Longarm said, "I'll ask, when I catch up with whoever might be left. One of the bodies in the river had that bright checkered shirt, right?"

Walt shook his head, dunked his doughnut, and replied, "Nope. I'm ahead of you on that, if you're talking about the train crew's brag about hitting that one. Neither body recovered was dressed unusual, and the Farnsworth kid we hauled in from Ralston's last night died in a dark blue shirt. So, soon as I finish this sinker, guess who we're fixing to posse up after? I already put out an all-points on a strange rider in a red and black checkered shirt, who may or may not be wounded but figures to be armed and dangerous either way."

Longarm whistled softly and declared, "That sounds almost too good to be true. And there goes Baker's notion it could be old Markham his fool self."

Walt started to ask why, then nodded and decided on his own, "That would be a dumb way for a master criminal to dress up for a train robbery."

Then Walt snapped his fingers and added, "Hold on! What if someone was to put on a noisy shirt, just long enough to rob a train, for the very same reasons he put on a feed-sack mask?"

Longarm got to his feet, muttering, "There's too dang many what-ifs to this whole infernal flimflam without us coming up with any of our own, Walt. It's been nice talking to you, but I got some chores of my own to tend to at the Western Union."

He overtipped again as he paid off the fat gal, making her flutter her lashes at him and blush. When he got to the counter of the telegraph office across the way, the somewhat slimmer but still well-padded little blonde on the far side asked, "Where were you last night around nine? Out with some other hussy, I'll bet!"

He regarded her warmly as he assured her he'd never noticed she was a hussy before. It would have been stupid to ask her how she knew he hadn't been at his hotel that early after moonrise, so he never did. He told her, "I had to ride down to the site of a killing with other lawmen, Miss Billie. I didn't get back till way later than nine. Now I got to wire my own office all about it. But before I do, has anyone anywhere sent any messages for me since last we discussed calling it a day?"

She sniffed, reached under the counter, and produced a wad of six or eight telegrams, saying, "Never mind when I get off work around here. The one from Denver just came in a few minutes ago."

He said he'd read a message from his own boss before he'd read any other, no matter when it arrived. He tore it open, read Billy Vail's terse wire, and confided to the buxom blonde, "That seems settled then. My boss wasn't impressed by my last progress report. He thinks I'm expending too much time and effort on a cold trail. So he's ordering me back down to Denver *poco tiempo*."

She looked as if someone had just punched her low and dirty and murmured, "Oh, then I reckon that's the end of the story, no matter what time a girl might get off work around here, huh?"

He said, "I ain't as sure I'm done here as my boss seems to feel. For openers, I still have to bring him up to date on two recent captures, and I'd be a fool to leave before I found out who and what that sheriff's posse might come back with."

She only looked a tad more hopeful as she asked, "Oh, will you be riding back into town no later than, say, nine then?"

He said, "I'm not riding with any posse. I only said I'd stick around till . . . six o'clock, didn't you say, Miss Billie?"

She blushed and said, "Don't go putting words or anything else in a girl's mouth, you fresh thing."

So he picked up a pad and pencil and proceeded to get back on the job, seeing she seemed one of those gals who played kid games long after they should have grown up.

As he wrote on, paying no attention to her as she tapped a toe on the far side of the counter, she suddenly blurted out, "Look, if you're not too proud to come back, later . . . "

So he had a pretty good notion he wouldn't be headed right back to Denver, no matter how things turned out up this way.

Having finished for now at the telegraph office, Longarm found himself sitting on the steps out front in the early morning light, reading answers to some of the other wires he'd sent far and wide the day before, when the posse went by in a cloud of dust. Nobody even slowed but Stump, who reined in long enough to call out an invite.

Longarm waved Stump on, yelling, "I can't. Got questions to ask here in town!"

Stump rode on after the others. Longarm rose, muttering, "Dusty assholes," as he crossed to the upwind side of the street, holding his breath and putting the bunched-up wires away for now.

171

He strode up to the Forbisher house, a mite surprised by its pink siding as he got his first good look by daylight. He opened the gate in the picket fence just as the doc popped out his front door with his black bag. He smiled uncertainly at Longarm and decided, "Oh, you're one of those lawmen from last night, right?"

Longarm identified himself and explained, "I have some more questions I'd like Thorp Ralston to clear up for us, if he's feeling more sensible this morning, Doctor."

Forbisher nodded and said, "As a matter of fact my old woman is serving him a good breakfast this very minute. Let yourself in and just go on back to the kitchen, past the clinic you must remember from last night. I have to visit a way sicker patient now."

Longarm moved out of the older man's way, but asked just what shape Thorp Ralston might be in now. The sage-looking G.P. shrugged and said, "Give it a couple of days and he'll have died of blood poisoning or feel good as new. He's had a good night's rest. The wound in his thigh was superficial, and I did my best to debride and irrigate every bit of injured tissue."

Longarm asked what caliber slug had injured it. The doc shook his head and said, "Can't say for certain. I just told you it was a simple flesh wound. The bullet passed mostly through muscle and fat, more fat than muscle, and just kept going. From the track it did leave I'd guess it was a .32 at the most. Might have been even smaller, say a .22 varmint-plunker, and now I really have to leave, Deputy Long."

Longarm apologized for keeping the busy sawbones from his appointed rounds, and moved on up the steps to the front door. The master of the house had said to go on in. But Longarm had been raised stricter than that. So he twisted the chime handle till, sure enough, the doc's sweet old woman came to open up and invite him back for breakfast.

He said he'd already eaten but might have room for more coffee. So they went on back, where old Ralston sat at the table, looking a lot less pale and wall-eyed, with a heroic plate of grub and a mighty big mug of Arbuckle in front of him.

As the two men shook and the old lady moved back to her monstrous notion of a kitchen range, Longarm was glad he'd already had breakfast. For there were limits to even his cast-iron digestion, and he saw she considered cornmeal hush puppies and turnip greens, deep fried in sowbelly grease, just the ticket for a hearty breakfast.

Longarm got rid of his hat and sat across the pine table from the wondrously recovered squatter, saying, "Ain't much new to report since you rid in last night on Midnight, Thorp. I understand your neighbors are tending your stock till you're up and around, and most everyone else who heard your sad story is out searching for the one who got away."

As the doc's old woman placed a mug of Arbuckle in front of him, all fucked up with cream and sugar whether he wanted it or not, he thanked her with a nod and said, "I don't expect them to find any other members of that four-man gang of train robbers alive. Two bobbed down the Big Thompson. That one in the checkered shirt was hit, hard enough to notice, a long hard ride from your place. So he'd have surely holed up or died miles to the north, once he made it into the hills worth mention. It just wouldn't have made any sense for a wounded man to push past all the natural hideouts you have to ride clean around to get down here from up yonder. That leaves young Farnsworth, who did make it all the way to your cabin last night, and we know *he* never rid on afterwards."

Thorp Ralston stuffed his face with another greasy hush puppy and, talking with his mouth filled, suggested, "I likely heard the Farnsworth boy's pony running off. I told you it was dark and confusing, even before I caught a round. The critter was doubtless spooked by all the gunplay, and you know how ponies are."

Longarm nodded soberly and said, "I've known some well in my time. I've never met a sensible pony yet who'd run far, saddled and bridled, once it knew where other members of its species were pastured at ease with room for one more."

He took a sip, managed not to let his feeling show as the sweet old lady watched him from over near her bubbling cannibal pot, and explained, "It makes more sense to me that Rafe Farnsworth rode it in along the post road so's its hoof marks could get erased by more recent arrivals. It left no sign leaving on account it never left. You were here, getting patched, whilst the rest of us were poking about down yonder like chickens with our heads cut off. So who's to say the mighty weary mount young Farnsworth rid down from the Big Thompson wasn't standing there amid all the others, staring back at us in plain sight?"

Mrs. Forbisher had been paying at least as much attention. So it was she who said, "That young train robber might have been in the very act of switching saddle and bridle to a fresh mount when poor young Timmy heard him. But in that case shouldn't the saddle have been somewhere in the vicinity when the rest of you young men rode in?"

Longarm nodded and replied, "Yessum. It wasn't. That's not saying it couldn't have been stored neatly with all the other gear in the tack shed. Nobody but your breakfast guest here, and the murdered Tim Cagney of course, was in any position to say so last night."

The man across the table gasped, "Suffering snakes, I'm commencing to see the light! That fugitive as gunned poor Tim wasn't expecting Tim or me to be there when he rid in bold as brass. For ain't it been established that professor was using the old Whipple place as some sort of outlaw way station before I moved on to the property more opensome?"

Longarm nodded and replied, "That works even better once you read a wire I just got from the Bureau of Land Management. Seems the last man to hold lawful title to the spread, Levi Whipple, was another Galvanized Yankee, restored to full civil rights when he agreed to fight Indians for the Union, the same as Hiram Paget, the Reconstructed

Rebel who held title to that other homestead the gang was using, down along the Boxelder."

Mrs. Forbisher said, "Well, I never! Didn't someone tell me that evil professor leading all those young boys into temptation was yet another confounded slavocrat?"

Longarm nodded soberly but went on staring at the other gent in the small kitchen as he replied, "Yessum, and I have to admit that part had me mighty mixed up. For although I've looked high and although I've looked low, I just haven't been able to find one mortal soul who's ever laid eyes on Jethro Markham since he died, officially, in his lifer's cell at Iowa State Prison."

The older gent who didn't fit Markham's description at all suggested, "What if he lit out for parts unknown as soon as he found out you were at all interested in his whereabouts, Longarm? I know it would give *me* a pair of mighty itchy feet if I thought you suspected me of anything more serious than poor church attendance!"

Longarm chuckled and assured him, "So far I haven't a single federal offense on you, old son. As I told you, sitting down, I only came to clear up a few details the local sheriff's department seems to have accepted as is."

Mrs. Forbisher said, "Oh, good. I was afraid for a minute you thought the doctor and me were harboring criminals in our root cellar. Are you both sure you don't want one of these hush puppies? They don't keep well once they cool off, and it'd be a shame to just throw them out when I pour this grease back in the jars."

Thorp Ralston shoved back from her table, saying, "Lord love you, ma'am, I couldn't swallow another if my life depended on it. Longarm here was about to tell us what he couldn't swallow about that young cuss as killed the Cagney boy last night."

Longarm nodded and said, "It might not have confused me as much if some sneak thief hadn't helped himself to Rafe Farnsworth's sixgun amid all that confusion. No matter how I try, I just can't picture his pistol. I mean, Tim

175

Cagney was shot in the heart with, say, a .44 or .45, the same as Farnsworth. Yet you were pinked with a .22, a .32 at most, or could it have been the tine of your hired hand's pitchfork?"

Longarm had naturally drawn his own .44–40, under the table, before he'd spoken so disrespectfully to an elder. But he saw he'd placed too much confidence in age and leg wounds when the dumpy cuss was suddenly out of his chair and behind the sweet old lady, with her poor frail neck in the grip of one elbow and a nickel-plated derringer shoved up behind one of her earlobes as he snarled, "You're too smart by half. But I'm way smarter, and there's two rounds of .45-short in this little darling, handy as it was to carry concealed!"

Longarm sat frozen as he softly replied, "You were never smart, and gunning your last desperate follower and the only other witness to his desperation only concealed you overnight. It's over, Professor, or should I call you Hiram Paget, as your mamma and the state of Iowa doubtless did long ago and far away? "

The exposed born loser snarled, "It ain't over. I want you to haul that sixgun out from under that table and place it ever so gentle on the planks betwixt us, with the grips towards me, of course."

Mrs. Forbisher sobbed, "Don't do it, Deputy Long! As things now stand, he knows that if he kills me you'll drop him right on top of me! But if you surrender your weapon he'll be able to kill us both with impunity!"

Longarm sighed and said, "I suspect he'd rather use bullets, ma'am. But anyone can see you've got more sense about such matters than our master criminal and his even dumber pupils. So what we got here seems a Mexican standoff, with the odds favoring somebody dropping by to break the stalemate long before this dimwit can come up with anything else to ante up. So how's about it, Dimwit? I just told you I didn't have federal charge *número uno* on you, and a good lawyer might get you off with Life at Hard if he can convince a Colorado judge and jury you shot Tim Cagney in the second degree as well as the heart."

The desperate killer between the old lady and her hot kitchen range whined, "I'm lighting out on Midnight, right now, before that posse gets back from the fool's errand I sent 'em on in my clever way. I'm taking your gun and this lady with me, just a ways, as a hostage. That's unless you'd rather see me spatter her brains all over the ceiling. So what's it going to be?"

Longarm shoved his chair back from the table to lift his own weapon into view, holding it by the cylinder with its grips aimed harmlessly at Paget. As he placed it gently on the bare pine between them he said, "Before I let go, entire, I want your word as a soldier who fought for both sides."

So Hiram Paget gave it. But as Longarm let go the sixgun and leaned back from it, the sweet but smart old lady wailed, "Oh, Lord, now you've done it, young man!"

The rascal holding her hauled his wicked little weapon out from behind her ear to swing it Longarm's way, saying, "You're right, ma'am. *Adios, amigo mio!*"

Then things got mighty confusing in the cramped quarters of the Forbisher kitchen for a spell. For even as the professor fired, Longarm was going over backwards, chair and all, as he clawed for his own belly gun in his vest pocket. He landed on his back and rolled across the kitchen floor to come up in a far corner with his derringer as the professor dove forward for the sixgun on the table, letting go the sweet and frail-looking Mrs. Forbisher.

So she, in turn, whirled around to snatch up her big pot of sowbelly grease and toss the boiling contents over their mutual enemy as if she aimed to put Hiram Paget out like a kitchen fire.

It didn't work quite that sedately. Boiling oil being way hotter than boiling water, the old Yankee gave a whoop worthy of all Little Crow's warriors put together as the hot hog-renderings ran down his back to settle, still smoking, in the crotch of his pants.

Losing all interest in any other thing in the universe, the dreadfully scalded villain fell to the floor at Longarm's feet to flop about on the greasy flooring like a fish being pan-fried alive. He probably felt like one. So Longarm kicked him in the head to calm him a mite as Mrs. Forbisher poured a pitcher of buttermilk over him, murmuring, "My land, what a mess. But I had to do something. Do you think I've killed him, Deputy Long?"

Longarm shook his head and assured her, "He ought to live long enough to stand trial, ma'am. Won't matter after they find him guilty, see?"

Chapter 14

Once Longarm made it back to Denver, he was told out front that he was wanted in the back when and if he ever showed up again. So he lit a cheroot along the way, in the vain hope that Billy Vail might have finally sprung for an infernal ashtray to go with that otherwise comfortable visiting chair.

Billy hadn't. Longarm flicked some ash on the rug, ground it in with a boot heel, and sat down, meeting Vail's glare with a mild smile and asking, "What has you so pissed this morning, Boss? Didn't you get my wired-in report, and didn't I tell you I might have to help the local law tidy up some loose ends up Lyons way?"

Vail said, "You did, last week as a matter of fact. But before you explain what you've been up to all this time, explain some of the shit you must have left out of that mighty confusing night letter. You had so many names to keep straight in my head, it felt like I was reading a damned old Russian novel."

Longarm grimaced and replied, "How do you think *I* felt? I had to *write* the son-of-a-bitching report. All you, me, and the Justice Department have to keep in mind, in the end, is the cheersome way it all panned out. The only federal angle was that holdup down in the Indian Nation and old Isaak Parker and the Fort Smith Federal District can hang those poor nitwits. Colorado claims jurisdiction over all the other shit the so-called master criminal and his so-called pupils pulled, and of course the murder of Lucky Lem Corrigan was a purely county crime."

Vail asked, "What about Iowa State and flight across state lines to avoid justice?"

Longarm grimaced and said, "You must have been confused by all them names, most of 'em switched around like the rubber pea under walnut shells. Nobody on neither side did nothing wrong in Iowa, Billy. The real Jethro Markham, serving life, died natural in his cell and they buried him out back. So nobody should have been looking for him to begin with. We were simply the victims of a bullshit artist."

He took a drag on his smoke, blew some thoughtfully out his nostrils, and continued, "They let Hiram Paget out the next day, just as they said they might. He'd served his short sentence, as a model prisoner with time coming to him. So there's no Iowa charge on that. It's hard to say just where or when he decided to tell everyone he was really the dead Jethro Markham. The how-come is easier. As Hiram Paget he was a pathetic figure of fun. Not even a stupid young crook was about to pay for lessons from a man who'd been nailed on his very first attempt at armed robbery."

Vail waved his own reeking smoke in a circle, as if he meant to throw a rope noose or wanted to have his own say. When Longarm let him, Vail said, "I savvy all the shit about a lazy homesteader and failed crook setting up some sort of con game as someone way more famous. I can even see how he got young squirts who'd never met the more notorious Jethro Markham to lay out good money for bum steers, with the confusing results you reported. Where you lost me was the stuff about Sioux risings and Galvanized Yankees. Markham rode for the South, but he was never captured during the war, was he?"

Longarm shook his head and replied, "Nope. The real Jethro Markham shouldn't have known this part of the West all that well either. So once I noticed not one but two Colorado homestead claims filed by old-timers who might have known one another riding against Little Crow in Wisconsin and Minnesota . . . "

"By jimmies, a lot of the new settlers the Sioux were pestering that time were Scandinavian immigrants!" Vail said, adding, "Ain't Ralston a Swede name, as soon as you study on it?"

Longarm nodded and said, "Using Thorp as a first name makes it more so. Paget liked to mix up real names instead of making 'em up out of thin air. I wasn't able to determine who the dead Swedes he recalled of old might have been. Suffice it to say he'd left no records of anyone called Thorp Ralston in Kentucky or anywhere else I could think to wire. But as I was telling him, just before that sweet old lady scalded him half to death, the main thing as gave him away, once I noticed everyone else up yonder made more sense, was that nothing he told anyone under any title made much sense. He had the money to pay local help instead of tending chores you'd think a squatter with a small stud operation would be proud to do himself. I couldn't find a soul he'd ever sold a single pony. Yet he didn't seem to stealing anything neither. So where in thunder was he getting his pocket jingle?"

Vail nodded and said, "I read the part about the local law suspecting him early on and deciding he was harmless when they failed to see him ride off anywheres mysterious. By then he'd have known we were closing in too. So he graduated his pupils and sent 'em off to get rich in other parts. He even turned in that one boy who showed up late for classes, right?"

Longarm nodded and said, "Dwight Harcourt's been a big help and Kansas says they've no warrant on him, once Colorado's through with him. I'm pretty sure it was Rafe Farnsworth acting as the professor's dean of boys. His description matches that of the clown who tried to get

Judith Farnsworth to kill me. I never told her her own brother was such a total shit though. She and her poor sick father have enough on their plate."

Vail nodded and said, "I was wondering who you spent all that time with in that honeymoon suite atop the Peakview. How many times do I have to tell you the paymaster won't let us put such bullshit down as a legitimate travel expense, you randy cuss?"

Longarm smiled sheepishly and said, "I give you my word I went nowhere near Miss Judith Farnsworth once I learned both her lover and brother were dead. I let the county law have that joyous chore."

Vail shrugged and said, "Whatever. In any case, Undersheriff Baker is an old drinking pal of mine, and so I took the liberty of asking him when you failed to come home like a good little sheep. He reports you sure spent time up there in that honeymoon with some damned female, judging from all the moaning and groaning at night."

Longarm said, "I know. The poor little thing who had to handle all those bawdy wires said they made her blush red as any rose."

Watch for

LONGARM AND THE MONTANA MASSACRE

One hundred forty-sixth in the bold LONGARM series
from Jove

Coming in February!

WESTERNS!

at least a savings of $3.00 each month below the publishers price. Second, there is never any shipping, handling or other hidden charges—Free home delivery. What's more there is no minimum number of books you must buy, you may return any selection for full credit and you can cancel your subscription at any time. A TRUE VALUE!

Mail the coupon below

To start your subscription and receive 2 FREE WESTERNS, fill out the coupon below and mail it today. We'll send your first shipment which includes 2 FREE BOOKS as soon as we receive it.

Mail To:
True Value Home Subscription Services, Inc.
P.O. Box 5235
120 Brighton Road
Clifton, New Jersey 07015-5235

10494

YES! I want to start receiving the very best Westerns being published today. Send me my first shipment of 6 Westerns for me to preview FREE for 10 days. If I decide to keep them, I'll pay for just 4 of the books at the low subscriber price of $2.45 each; a total of $9.80 (a $17.70 value). Then each month I'll receive the 6 newest and best Westerns to preview Free for 10 days. If I'm not satisfied I may return them within 10 days and owe nothing. Otherwise I'll be billed at the special low subscriber rate of $2.45 each; a total of $14.70 (at least a $17.70 value) and save $3.00 off the publishers price. There are never any shipping, handling or other hidden charges. I understand I am under no obligation to purchase any number of books and I can cancel my subscription at any time, no questions asked. In any case the 2 FREE books are mine to keep.

Name _____

Address _____ Apt. # _____

City _____ State _____ Zip _____

Telephone # _____

Signature _____
(if under 18 parent or guardian must sign)
Terms and prices subject to change.
Orders subject to acceptance by True Value Home Subscription Services, Inc.